THE FOR AS YOU SEE TALES

Kathy (AE) Cox

authorHOUSE

AuthorHouse™
1663 Liberty Drive
Bloomington, IN 47403
www.authorhouse.com
Phone: 1 (800) 839-8640

© 2019 Kathy (AE) Cox. All rights reserved.

No part of this book may be reproduced, stored in a retrieval system, or transmitted by any means without the written permission of the author.

Published by AuthorHouse 10/11/2019

ISBN: 978-1-7283-3093-8 (sc)
ISBN: 978-1-7283-3092-1 (hc)
ISBN: 978-1-7283-3091-4 (e)

Library of Congress Control Number: 2019915951

Print information available on the last page.

Any people depicted in stock imagery provided by Getty Images are models, and such images are being used for illustrative purposes only. Certain stock imagery © Getty Images.

This book is printed on acid-free paper.

Because of the dynamic nature of the Internet, any web addresses or links contained in this book may have changed since publication and may no longer be valid. The views expressed in this work are solely those of the author and do not necessarily reflect the views of the publisher, and the publisher hereby disclaims any responsibility for them.

This is a work of fiction. Names, characters, businesses, places, events and incidents are either the products of the author's imagination or used in a fictitious manner. Any resemblance to actual persons, living or dead, or actual events is purely coincidental.

DEDICATION

I dedicate all of my short stories to the ones I love
and the ones who love me "unconditionally".

CONTENTS

Dedication v
Why Did The Chicken Cross The Road? xi

CHAPTER ONE
Animal Tales (Also Known As) Anthropomorphism

A Fish Tail 2
Calm, Cool, And Collected 4
Fair Game 6
Figuring It Out 9
Getting Back On Track 12
Hooking Horns 15
Howling At The Moon 18
In Remembrance Of Me 20
Junk Yard Dog 23
Momma Tiger, Papa Bear 25
Monkey Business 27
Not In A Million Years 29
One Bad Apple 32
See How Smart I Am 34
The Real Reason The Dodo Bird Is Extinct 36
Touché 38
Why Not Make It Fun? 41
Winter In The Cedars 43
A Dog's Tail 45

CHAPTER TWO
For The Young At Heart

A Story A Day Keeps The Doctor Away 48
All The Kings Horses And All The Kings Men 50
And This Too Shall Pass 52
Musical Chairs.. 55
Cause And Effect 57
Is It Contagious?...59
Lullaby 61
Not So Close 63
Planting A Seed 66
That's Not What I Wanted 68
The Bully 71
The Dragon And The Dragonfly 73
The Five Second Rule...76
The Story Teller 78
There Is A Snake In Our House 80
There Is A Storm Coming.. 82
Tis The Season 84
What's Different With Christmas This Year? 86
At The Equator, How Do They Know When It Is Christmas? 89
Campfire 92

CHAPTER THREE
For The Older Crowd

Doing Time.. 96
A Mother's Tears... 99
A Tale Of Two Sisters 101
An Up Hill Climb.. 103
Beanie This One Is For You... 105
Bringing Down This Old House... 107

Excuse Me Please 110

Don Pablo 113

How Special Are You?...116

That Was A Really Good Bad Dream 119

No Pain Means No Gain 121

Now, Was That So Hard?..................................... 124

Pandora's Box 127

Raining On Your Parade 130

Smelling The Roses.. 132

Genie In A Bottle.. 135

Swimming With The Fishes 137

That's Mine 140

The Extra Mile 144

The Hand Is Quicker Than The Eye 146

The Power Of Persuasion 149

The Year Of The Wolf.. 151

Will It Be Yes Or Will It Be No? 154

Workmanship... 157

I'm Covered... 160

One Last Dance 163

The Right Move 165

All In The Name Of The King............................167

Change 170

Sermon On The Mountain.................................173

Chopping Down A Cherry Tree 175

You Take The High Road And I'll Take The Low Road................177

CHAPTER FOUR
For My Eyes Only

A Little Known Fact About Gnomes 180

Being Human 183

Closing Out The Account 186

Cry Me A River 188

Defining Crazy 190
From A Frog To A Prince.. 192
If You Cut Me Do I Not Bleed?.............................. 195
It Is Only A Dream 198
My Wet Suit.. 201
Paul, Are There Really Any Angels?...................... 204
This Is What's Wrong With This World.................. 206
The Way I See It... 208
Why I Cry At Christmas 210
Is There A Weight Limit In Heaven?...................... 212
Divorce...214
What Is "FAMILY"?...216
Love Means Never Having To Say You're Sorry 218
Debridement (AKA) Picking A Scab....................... 220
Funny Is In The Eyes Of The Beholder 223
I Surrender.. 226
My Swan Song 228

About The Author.. 231

WHY DID THE CHICKEN CROSS THE ROAD?

PART TWO

A SHORT STORY

I would be willing to bet you, that if you were to ask a room full of people why any chicken would want to cross a road then I am convinced you would end up with a room full of people each with a different answer to that question. You would hear them maybe say that the chicken crossed the road because he ran out of sidewalk, or maybe he crossed the road because he needed something from the other side of town, or my favorite reply would be, because he was being chased by a very big bad mangy dog. Nope, the real reason the chicken crossed the road is simply because someone somewhere told him **not** to.

The reason I know this to be a factual statement is because just like the chicken, I too crossed the road only because my next door neighbor softly told me not to. It was a beautiful spring day, just perfect weather to be out in my back yard enjoying the smell of freshly cut grass floating in the air around me. Being a Saturday morning every male for miles around was out mowing his grass, so the sound of circling lawnmowers seemed to drown out all the other noises in my neighborhood. My back yard fence was a metal chain link one just like all the other houses on my block, the only difference between mine and all the rest was a very dense overgrowth of honeysuckle vines. Let me let you in on a little know secret about honeysuckle vines, not only do they have the sweetest smelling flowers which attract humming birds, bees and little children, they also seem to house a wide variety of snakes. If not for the snake factor the thought of cutting down those vines would never have crossed my mind. Even now to this day I enjoy sucking the sweet juice from a honeysuckle flower while it is still in full bloom.

My sweet elderly next door neighbor who had known me for only a short while now, saw me looking at the vines and noticed the hedge clippers that I was holding in my right hand so he walked over to me. With the softest and nicest of voices he pointed to the vines and said "Kathy, do you see that green vine mixed in with the honeysuckle vines?" I said "Yes". He matter of factually stated, "That's Poison Oak, you do not want to mess with that", and then he went back to mowing his yard.

I had never heard of anything called Poison Oak, the only Poison thing I had ever heard of was Poison Ivy and even then I had never had any contact with the plant, so I had no way of knowing what kind of mess I was fixing to get myself into.

Dressed in a shirt with no sleeves to cover my arms, and just daisy duke high cut short shorts to protect my legs, and nothing on my feet but open toed flip flops, I was dressed to tackle the clearing of my backyard fence. Lord only knows where Kelly was at that particular time probably at work the only thing for sure was he wasn't anywhere around close enough to stop me. Armfuls after armfuls of vines were hugged up close to my exposed skin as I bagged it and then walked the bags from my backyard to the front yard for trash pickup. The more I worked, the hotter I got, and the more I sweated the more open the pores in my skin became which only gave the Poison Oak easier access to all my body parts.

Needless to say it took about three months, two ER visits, several shots, four different Doctors, numerous prescriptions, all kinds of creams and countless sleepless nights, not to mention makeup to try and cover the whelps on my face, all because I never seem to be able to learn my lesson anyway except the hard way.

I never told my neighbor that he was the wisest man on the planet (even though I should have) and I never told him that I had Poison Oak from my head to my toes, but somehow I think he probably figured it out since every time after that when he saw me I was sweating bullets while wearing long sleeve shirts with long pants, socks and tennis shoes on. I even think I had Poison Oak on my ear drums. Talk about being miserable, that happened about 1984 and I am still carrying the scars of that one summers messed up adventure.

For as you see, The next time someone tells this chicken to stop and think twice about why I should be crossing the road, I would be willing to wager all I own with you that before I make my first step out, I will stop and look both ways, check out the wind speed and direction, look up at the sky for rain clouds, listen for thunder and lightning then make sure the stripe in the middle of the road I am crossing is dry and not just newly painted. Yep, I think I learned my lesson the hard way don't you? No matter how softly it is put to you, you should always, beyond a shadow of a doubt, **listen to what your elders have to say to you**.

End of Story

CHAPTER ONE

Animal Tales (Also Known As) Anthropomorphism

A Fish Tail

A SHORT STORY

Each spring, sometime in the later part of March, there is a stirring that begins way down deep in the Lake. All the commotion is brought about just to announce to all that the time has come again for the spawning ritual of the Rainbow Trout. Of course all the fish in the Lake are invited to the party, but the King and Queen of this event will always be reserved for the Lake Trout only.

Tammy and Thelma Trout wouldn't have been late for this year's festival even if both of their lives depended upon it, and so as they finished eating lunch the two Sisters got all dressed up and headed down to the deep end of the Lake. There they stopped swimming just about 10 feet from the outskirts of the crowd that had already begun to gather for the concert. Standing there they just stared out across the festival fairgrounds trying really hard to find a friend or two to dance with after the music started to play.

The stage was all set up and ready with drums and guitars in place, and the group of fish in front started clapping and chanting in the middle of the mosh pit by the time Tammy said, "Thelma,

THE FOR AS YOU SEE TALES

who are you looking for?" Thelma replied, "I was hoping to see Todd again this year. He sure was more than just a good time last year and I know it just won't be the same if he doesn't make it back to dance with me again." Then Thelma added, "Tammy do you have anyone in mind for your first dance?"

Tammy blushed as she said, "there was this one good looking hunk of fish that turned my head last year, and I think his name was Tony." Thelma questioned Tammy by saying, "girl, how are you going to locate just one fish from all the other hundreds of fish down there?" Tammy replied, "Sis, there he is, just look over there, don't you see him?" Thelma said, "Where is he? Point him out to me."

Tammy pointed over and out into the crowd and then said, "See him; he is the good looking one over there who is grinning from gill to gill." Thelma said, "oh yeah, he does stand out in a crowd. Now do you think you can help me spot Todd?" Tammy said, "Sure Sis what does he look like?" Thelma replied, "You know he shouldn't be that hard to find since he is missing half a spot on his left side." Tammy laughed as she said, "well Sis, you are going to need a little bit more than just your average amount of good luck finding him out there in all that sea of spots."

For as you see, nothing stands out better in a crowd of frowns than someone who has a really big smile on his face.

End of Story

Calm, Cool, And Collected

A SHORT STORY

South America is where they say the most abundant amount of insects in the world can be found. So I would imagine that South America is where there would also have to be an abundance of lizards just to keep the insects at bay. This is where my story comes into play.

Deep in the Amazon Rain Forest high up in the trees lives a pair of chameleons named Leo and Leon. Leo and Leon ruled the top most branch of their favorite tree. One day Leo, the thinner of the two lizards, couldn't stand it any longer he just had to ask Leon a question. Leo said, "Friend, why is it that you have no trouble at all getting all the bugs you want to eat where I have to nearly run them down just to be able to survive?" Leon lazily turned to Leo and said, "Well friend, just look at how different we are. I can sit completely still on this branch, while changing colors to easily blend into my surroundings, and then I can keep being this still all day if that is what it takes for the bugs to come within tongue striking distance of me. I make the food come to me, where you can't even stay still long enough for me to finish this conversation."

Leo replied, "you know you are absolutely right, I think the reason I can't stay still is because I am constantly worrying about where my next meal will come from, which in turn keeps the bugs far away from me making it harder then for me to catch them. I guess my worrying has made my life just one big vicious cycle." Leon said, "That's exactly what your problem is. If you will just learn to relax then the bugs around you will also relax and let their guard down, which will in turn makes your life a whole lot easier." Leo then told Leon that if he sees him even try to make a wrong move then he had his permission to swat him. So with Leon's help Leo never went hungry again, because if Leo even thought about moving an inch then Leon would stick his tongue out at Leo and double dog dared him to blink an eye.

For as you see, trying too hard and worrying about whether or not you will get what you want will always be the enemy of success, and the easiest way to get pregnant, especially when the doctor's say you can't have a baby, is to relax, tell yourself not to worry, and then go out and buy a new house, a new car, and a new boat. Because it never fails that when you can no longer afford to have a baby, one will miraculously seem to come your way.

End of Story

Fair Game

A SHORT STORY

Among the deepest reaches of the African Serengeti Plains lies a solemn plateau overlooking a vast area of flat land. On the open green plain all different varieties of grass eating animals have gathered together to celebrate the up and coming spring season, which God has set aside for the birth of their offspring. Soon the soft fresh green blades of grass will rise up too nestle and hide the little ones, safe and sound from the view of any would be predators.

Elmore, being the leader and oldest of the Lion pride had brought his oldest son Eli to the plateau overlooking the Serengeti for his first lesson on hunting. Elmore asked Eli to look out across the vast plain and tell him what he saw. Eli said, "Dad, I see every animal that lives around us, ones that we hunt and ones that we know not to hunt like the elephant." Elmore said, "Good observation Son, now tell me why we leave the elephant alone." Eli said, "I think it is because the elephant is so very big that we would have to work way too hard to take him down." Elmore replied, "That is surely part of the reason, but the most important reason is that when you take the time to count the elephant you will see that there are not more than just a handful of them left for us to hunt. So to be a wise and strong leader we should chose to only hunt the elephant when he is sick and dying, because if we do not choose to selectively hunt only certain elephants then soon they will all be gone forever."

Elmore then asked Eli to point to the animal that he would choose to hunt if he was asked to go down to the plains and hunt one of them for their supper. Eli replied, "Dad it wouldn't make a difference to me because I can catch anyone of them that I choose to at any time I decide to." His Dad said, "You are completely correct about your ability and power to hunt down any that you see, but because of that, you also have to take on the responsibility that goes along with having that power." Eli said, "What responsibility Dad? If I am hungry shouldn't I just take food as it comes to me?" His Dad roared, "no Son, there is no pride in hunting the smallest or the weakest in front of you, which are usually all the littlest ones.

That wouldn't give them the chance they need to grow up and feed you many years from now, and if their Mothers feel that their babies are all at risk, then they will move elsewhere to raise them which will then make us have to move right along with them just for our own survival. It makes much more sense to only hunt the older, less healthy adult males and leave the babies and their mothers alone." Eli said, "Dad that is a lesson and a choice I will always remember and promise to be true to." Elmore hugged his Son and let him know how proud he was of the lesson he had just learned and if he saw his younger brother he needed to send him over his way.

For as you see, there is a reason why hunting seasons open and close at a certain time. The rules exist to protect the animals we hunt and since man is #1 at the top of the list of predators on this planet he has a responsibility to abide by those rules and regulations. Unlawful Poachers do not kill for the meat and food, they only hunt for the profit and if they keep it up, then they will hunt themselves totally out of business and take the rest of us right along with them, because the closer the animals we hunt get to extinction by our hand, the closer our own extinction on this planet will become.

End of Story

Figuring It Out

A SHORT STORY

I'm cured, I'm cured, I really think I'm cured. No wait, No wait, I'm pretty sure I feel another story coming on. So just when you think you are cured of hypergraphia, out will pop another story from your head.

As with all good friends, when the time comes and you really need them, they always seem to be around. The same is true of your very closest relatives, because when the time comes and you need someone to bale you out of a jam, no one else does that better than someone who was born to love you. So for the life of me I can never understand why the ones who love us the most are always the ones whose advice we tend to ignore the most. The point of this story has hit very close to home for me in more ways than one, since I too, am guilty of ignoring my Mommas and friends wise and greatly needed advice.

Some of the driest and most arid land on earth can be found in Death Valley, California, but even with such harsh climate, the valley is still teaming with an abundance of wild life. Death Valley happens to be home to a couple of young mountain lions named "Fast and Bright". It wasn't hard to figure out which one was Fast, because every creature around couldn't outrun him, and with Bright at his side they never went hungry. Both of them were feeling the strength and courage that only being young can supply. Being teenagers for them was easy, so the only hard part of growing up was constantly trying to prove to the rest of the male mountain lions that they had finally come of age and needed the respect that maturity brings.

At the edge of the mountain range rose a steep rocky cliff that overhung a dry creek bed at the base of the mountain. One evening as the sun was going down the two young lions decided to spend the night lying in the cool soft sand of the creek bed. As they lay there they heard a familiar roar coming from the rock above. It was an old friend of their Mothers and one who had lived in the desert all his life.

The old mountain lion roared another "hello" to the two young lions and then as they answered him back he asked them if they planned on spending the night down in the creek bed. The two politely replied "yes", and it was then that the older lion reminded them that their Mother had always told them not to sleep there. Fast and Bright roared back that they weren't afraid of anything and Bright then added that he had never really understood why she wouldn't want them to stay nice and cozy sleeping in the dry creek bed. They both declined him when he offered to let them sleep with him up on the rocks for the night. Then the two added that they had hear the lecture he was giving them at least one thousand times when their Mom wanted to be overly protective and didn't want them to have their freedom or grow up too soon.

The older lion just shook his head and then left them alone. Around midnight the sky started roaring off in the distance. Bright woke up and told Fast that their Mom had warned them about the sky that roared, but Fast just rolled over and told him to go back to sleep. A few hours later another roar could be heard in the distance and it wasn't but a few more seconds before the roar was followed

THE FOR AS YOU SEE TALES

by a wave of uncontrollable water rushing down the dry creek bed. The water swept the two of them downstream and it took all they could do just to crawl out of the water and up to higher ground.

The old lion saw what had happened to the teenagers, but was helpless to assist them until they got out of the stream of water and climbed up to where he was waiting. They both were totally out of breath when the older asked if they were ok. They both said that they were Ok, but maybe, just maybe, sleeping in the creek bed wasn't such a good idea after all. The older lion just smiled and said, "I guess neither one of you will need to be told the one thousand and one time about how dangerous the dry creek bed can really be." They both said, "You got that right".

For as you see, some people only learn from experiencing danger face to face. So if hearing something "one thousand times" doesn't sink in good enough to protect you, <u>then yes</u>, you will have to hear it one thousand and one times, because I care.

End of Story

Getting Back On Track

A SHORT STORY

It's time to go back to the jungle. I have pined away long enough for my first attempt at getting my book published. I was so close, yet so far away, all at the same time. I am not the kind of person to just sit around and wait for something that I want, although I realize it won't be just like I need it to be, unless I do develop a little bit more patience. I think one of the reasons I do not have any children today is simply because I would have to wait 9 months for one to be born. Patience is truly a virtue that I am somewhat lacking in.

Deep down in the deepest darkest jungle, just along the river bank grows a grove of date trees. Every monkey for miles around knows at what time of year they should come to the river, if they wanted to find the trees hanging with their branches full of sweet, ripened in the sun, dates. The fruit from this grove of date trees is as sweet as any candy man has ever made, and so the treat the trees offer up is well worth the waiting and the miles the monkeys will have to travel just to enjoy their treat.

THE FOR AS YOU SEE TALES

Each day for about a week, Mat and Mark would go down at the break of dawn to the river just to check, and see if the dates were ripe enough to eat, and each day they would have to look at each other and say "not just yet". The blessed day came for the dates on the trees to reach their peak of ripening, and that announcement could be heard coming at dawn from all of the monkey's loudly rejoicing for miles around. Mat ran into Mark's room and said to his friend, "wake up sleepy head, can't you hear the ruckus coming from the grove down by the river? The dates are finally ready and if we do not hurry then all the big, sweet, plump ones will be all gone before we can even get there." Mark moaned as he turned over in his bed and told Mat that he had better go down to the river all by himself.

Mat was very concerned about his friend when he said, "What's wrong with you Mark?" Mark groaned and then told Mat that his stomach was hurting and he was sick and couldn't get out of bed right at that moment. Once again he told Mat to just go on without him.

As Mat turned to leave he asked Mark why he thought he was in so much pain. He said, "Was it something you ate, or do you have a stomach virus?" It was then that Mark confessed and told him that he had made an earlier trip down to the river the night before and sat there and ate as many of the green dates as he could put into his mouth. Mat felt so sorry for his friend that he told him he would bring him back some of the ripened dates, just so he would have a few to eat after he felt better. Mark just told him not to waste his time, because the way he felt at the moment let him know it might be years before he would ever want to look at another date let alone eat another one.

Curiosity took hold so before he shut the bedroom door behind him to leave for the river Mat said, "Friend, why did you make yourself so sick? You knew that the dates weren't ready for us to eat, so why did you eat them?" All Mark could say was that the temptation was overwhelmingly immense and the waiting seemed eternal.

For as you see, Nothing worth having is obtained in haste, and without patience most of the time you will find that getting in a hurry will only leave you disappointed with a really bitter taste in your mouth.

End of Story

Hooking Horns

A SHORT STORY

"This is how the story went", is the first line Ted wrote in his journal that day, and as he wrote on, page after page, he came to realize that this story would be one for the record books. This story would surpass all that he had written before, and because of that, he pondered long and hard on each word that he wrote. So in case you haven't already guessed I would just like for you to know that this is how the story went.

Home on the range meant a lot to the boys, Mr. Rogers' two prize bulls "Rick and Nick" that is. They had worked really hard and managed to stay relatively happy bulls most of their lives while living on Mr. Rogers' farm. They always had the run of the pasture, the barnyard and they of course had the hay filled little red barn all to themselves. They were <u>happy</u> and as you well know, a happy bull is a content bull. Even when there was a lot of hard work pulling the plow in the field, Rick and Nick did it with a smile on their faces.

Rick looked at Nick one day just about sundown, and asked him what time it was. Nick replied that he thought it was just about suppertime. Rick commented about how fast time flies when you are having fun. After agreeing with him about the speed in which the day had flown they both finished the row of ground they were plowing and then they both headed back to the barn to call it a night and go off to bed. As they rounded the corner of their little red barn and opened the door to go in, both of them were stopped dead in their tracks. There standing in the middle of their barn was another bull. Politely they asked the newcomer what his name was and politely he answered, my name is "Your Highness". Rick and Nick couldn't say a word.

If they said, "Hi, Your Highness, nice to met you" would that be the correct thing to say? Nothing they could think of to say at the moment would seem to be coming out right, so both of them just looked at each other and then decided to just be quite and go on off to bed.

That night was awkward to say the least, Rick and Nick whispered back and forth to each other in an effort to try and figure out why there was a new bull in their midst, and all the whispering they did just made the newcomer feel that much more unwelcome. The next morning was just as awkward as the night before and Your Highness took every look and every unspoken word between them to mean that they didn't like him. It wasn't long before Your Highness started to make changes, ones that would make him happy, but not really caring about what the other two thought about the changes he had made.

First he changed little things like the way the hay was stacked in the barn, and then he decided the roosters were no longer welcome to come and wake them up in the morning, and worst of all he shut the windows so no noise could be heard coming from Mr. Rogers' house. As the differences between them grew bigger and bigger, so did the number of changes Your Highness made around the barn and barnyard. And then one day it happened, right there in front of Mr. Rogers' face and it wasn't a pretty sight. Three grown bulls, all with their horns locked in a free for all, knock down, drag out fight, tossing hay, chickens, and farm equipment to all four corners

THE FOR AS YOU SEE TALES

of the little red barn. Mr. Rogers knew there wouldn't be any way he could stop them, so all he did was shut the door and hope the barn would still be standing when they finally tired themselves out and finished acting like angry bullheaded bulls.

It wasn't until sunrise the next day before all the dust had settled and the fur had quit flying around the little red barn. Only then did Mr. Rogers venture to slowly open the door and peek inside. As he stood there in the doorway, his mouth open wide in astonishment, he became speechless just for a moment. There sitting drinking coffee together as if nothing had even happened, were all three of his bulls. Stunned Mr. Rogers asked, "Well did the three of you finally work out all your differences?" All three of them nodded "yes" simultaneously, and then offered Mr. Rogers a cup of coffee. Next, Rick and Nick proceeded to introduce their new roommate Mick (formally know as "Your Highness") to their lifelong friend and owner Mr. Rogers. The next words out of Mr. Rogers's mouth were, "Nice to meet you Mick, but you know, you three still have to clean up the mess you managed to make in this barn." But you know from the looks of it, the mess was well worth the clean up fun they were facing.

For as you see, sometimes it takes two people hooking horns, having words of disagreement with each other, to finally bring out the harmony between them.

End of Story

Howling At The Moon

A SHORT STORY

Nothing is prettier than a full summer moon shining brightly onto the Nevada desert. As usual Cleo was sitting on his rock, the one that he occupies almost every Saturday when the weather is permitting. Cleo wasn't the scraggliest coyote in the bunch, but he also wasn't the most handsome one either. All of a sudden out of the blue Cecile came up and sat down beside him. Cleo was startled at first, because he was quite use to having no one else around when he started his howling at the moon, but a visit from his friend was certainly a welcome one.

Cleo said, "Hi friend, what brings you up here tonight? Do you just want to hear me howl or do you want to join me in a chorus or two? If you'll stay I'll give you a few singing lessons?" Cecile just laughed and replied, "Cleo, you are the one who needs singing lessons and if I had the time I would stay and give you a few pointers on the rite of howling. I hate to say it but I am just passing by, and I felt the need to stop and ask you a personal question." Cleo couldn't help but ask Cecile what question it could be that he needed to ask of him. So Cecile said, "Cleo, my friend, why do you sit here and waste your time howling at the moon all night when you could be sleeping instead?"

Cleo was just a little bit taken back by the question, since of course he didn't think that his howling was a waste of time at all, so he said, "Let me ask you a question and then I will answer yours." Cecile said, "Sure buddy what do you want to know." Cleo put his hands on his hips and then asked, "Cecile, why do you spend almost every Saturday chasing those ground gophers in and out of their holes? You know you really won't do a thing with them except let them go even if you are fortunate enough to catch one of them?" Cecile replied, "Are you really asking me why I want to play my full round of 18 hole gopher golf?" Cleo said, "Yes, I just didn't know exactly what you called it. So let me ask you again, why do you waste your time playing **gopher golf**?" Cecile couldn't help but laugh when he said, "it isn't a waste of time for me, and it is what I call fun." Cleo said, "well, then there you have it, my howling at the moon is also what I call fun.

So you see you answered your own question for me. I just waste my time at night where you waste yours during the day." As Cecile was getting up to leave when Cleo stopped him and said, "Cecile you might want to stay just a little bit longer, because I see Gladys just off in the distance and if I'm not very badly mistaken then you are in luck tonight friend, because I am pretty sure that she has brought a girlfriend along with her. Now hold onto your ears, because it is time for me to start howling out the tune "Chantilly Lace", and just so you will know, that is the song she likes the most and fortunately enough for me it is also the one I love to sing to her."

For as you see, howling at the moon or just playing gopher golf, it really doesn't matter what you love to waste your time doing, because as long as you are having fun, then truly no time is wasted.

End of Story

In Remembrance Of Me

A SHORT STORY

Even as little monkeys the two brothers were both totally different. Mike the oldest would give you the shirt off his back, while Todd would give you what you wanted, but in the same breath he would ask for something in return. They were both grown Fathers of their own when it became time for their Dad to pass away and leave them his very large coconut grove. The coconuts their Father grew were the best coconuts you could find in the Jungle, so when it became time to pick them, every monkey for miles around would make sure they were the first in line to get some of the coconuts.

Each of the two brothers were given their equal share of the grove, and then even with cutting it in half they both had enough of a crop of coconuts that they could say they were rich monkeys. Mike knew it was almost time to harvest the coconuts, but he also knew that he didn't have the time or effort it would take for him to gather all that his Dad had grown by himself, and so he decided to advertise his share of the crop in the local paper. The ad read, "I am having a pick as many as you can in a day sale. Mike's coconut

THE FOR AS YOU SEE TALES

grove". His brother Todd was more than just a little bit upset with Mike, since he felt as if Mike was just giving his coconuts away, and if he was a wise monkey then he would just save all of his coconuts and wait until the food supply got scarce, and then he could increase the price for his crop three fold. Mike insisted on the sale so he told his Brother that he was going to have the sale come rain or shine, so maybe he should put up a rope just so no one would go over onto his part of the grove when they came to pick the coconuts.

The day came for the sale and when the gate to the grove was opened there were more monkeys there than you could shake a stick at. Todd had put up a partition between the two groves and stopped anyone who ventured too far onto his side. When the time came for the gatherers to pay up, Mike just asked each and every one of them just exactly what his Dad had charged them for the coconuts. He wasn't surprised when almost all of them said that his Dad had given them the coconuts free of charge if they would just say a little prayer for him and his family the next time they went to church. Mike said, "That sounds like a real deal to me.

I would only like to request one more thing of you. I would like to ask that you gather enough coconuts to help feed your neighbor if they aren't able to get out and pick any for themselves." Every one of them said it would be their pleasure to do that for him, and they would tell anyone they met about how gracious his gift of kindness was.

Winter came and the food supply got scarce. That was when Todd decided to sell the abundance of coconuts he had stored up and not given away. The price was more than most working monkeys could afford, but if you are hungry you will find a way to pay the price. All the coconuts looked good on the outside, but when they were opened it was found that beetles had bored into each and every one of them, and because of the beetles the stored coconuts were all dried up and mildewed on the inside. Todd had to refund all the money he had collected and found himself in the very same predicament, since he had also thought the coconuts would feed him all winter long to. The two Brothers made it through the winter together, but when spring came, and the new addition to the church gym was finished and dedicated the plaque read, "this addition is dedicated to a great monkey and friend, Mike", which just happens to hang just a few feet away from his Dad's memorial plaque.

For as you see, once you are no longer here, all that will remain of you are the memories that your friends and loved ones carry with them. How do you want them to remember you?? Will it be as a true humanitarian or will it be as the world's biggest old bah humbug.

End of Story

Junk Yard Dog

A SHORT STORY

Night and day Chester guarded the wrecked cars that were piled up one on top of each other inside the fenced in yard that his owner had entrusted him to guard. One day when the owner came by to feed and water Chester, as he always did, his owner didn't just pet him and then walk away, this time he stayed and told Chester that he had just bought the two adjacent lots and was going to expand his wrecked car business, and since he knew it would be too much area for Chester to guard all by himself he told Chester he would be getting a new friend to help him guard it all.

Chester didn't know what to say so he just wagged his tail and then asked to be petted just a little bit longer. It wasn't long before his new friend arrived and the moment he jumped out of the car, Chester knew that they would hit it off and be very good friends. His owner introduced the new dog by saying "Chester this is Mack." Mack immediately started making a good first impression with Chester. Mack let Chester always take the lead when they walked around the fence and he would always wait until Chester decided which bowl he wanted at supper time before Mack would eat out of the one Chester didn't choose.

It wasn't long before Mack started asking Chester some questions about the cars they were there to guard. Mack said that if these were all wrecked cars and trucks, then why did their owner find a need to have them guard the junk car parts. Chester said that some of the car parts were worth more than others; because some of the cars were worth more than a hundred thousand dollars brand new, so even being wrecked they still were worth quite a bit of money. Then Mack asked Chester what had caused the cars to end up all wrecked in the first place. Chester pointed to one of the cars and said that the driver had ran a stop sign, then he pointed to another and said that its driver had tried to out run a train and then another one hadn't seen the other car beside him when he decided to change lanes.

Chester then said, "even if they call them "Accidents" they are all still humans just being human and making mistakes." Mack then swore that he would never be caught doing anything like that. Chester warned him not to be so sure of that, because accidents do happen unintentionally, that is why they call them accidents.

That night after dark, Mack heard someone open the gate and enter the yard. Mack started running towards the man and just before he attacked Chester stopped him and told him that the man coming through the gate was the owner's son. Mack said, "Opps, my mistake." Chester replied, "Well now, tell me, how does it feel to be human?" Mack just grinned.

For as you see, being human means making mistakes. Some of us will own up to our mistakes, while others will just hit and run. Accident or not, it is still humans making mistakes and being human.

End of Story

Momma Tiger, Papa Bear

A SHORT STORY

The trail around the mountain was a steep and narrow one, only wide enough to let one creature travel it at any given point in time. Usually that didn't pose a problem since most of the animals that traveled it to get from one valley to the other got along with each other. The night travelers only used it at night and the daytime travelers would go single file across the mountain during the day.

One day the unexpected happened at the break of dawn, half way along the mountain side a Momma Tiger with her cubs going up the trail came face to face with a Papa Bear and his cubs coming down the mountain towards the valley below. The Momma Tiger immediately came to the defensive stance and growled as she confronted the Papa Bear. The Papa Bear instantly rose up on his hind legs and let out a loud roar. Each one of them stood their ground and dared the other to even try and take another step forward. The passion with which they defended their young could be heard all the way down the mountainside and all the way up to the top of its summit. Every animal for miles around shook from fear of what would happen next.

After several minutes of confrontation the growling and roaring quieted down just long enough for the Momma Tiger to see past the Papa Bear and that is when she noticed the fear and distress that their fighting had made on the Bear Cubs behind him. It was only then that the Papa Bear noticed the Tiger Cubs sitting down visible shaking behind their Mother.

Momma Tiger stopped growling and started talking to the Bear, she said, "Sir maybe there is a way for us to end our arguing without anyone else getting hurt". Papa Bear said, "I will listen to what you have to say, because I am starting to get pretty hoarse from all my roaring." Momma Tiger then said, "even though I can growl at you all day long that will not get either one of us off the side of this mountain anytime soon. So this is what I would like to suggest.

I know it is easier to go down this mountain; in fact it is a whole lot easier to go down than it would be to climb back up it. I know it is pretty close to the time for you to take your troops and hibernate for the winter, so if you will agree to it then I will turn around and head my group back down the mountain before I try and go back up it any further.

Papa Bear replied, "I will be very thankful to you if you chose to do that for me, because I am starting to get very tired of standing here." Momma Tiger turned around and they all regrouped at the bottom of the mountain. Now each time they cross paths with each other not one growl or roar is heard, only a friendly nod of their heads is gestured out of respect for one another.

For as you see, there is nothing fiercer than a Mother Tiger or a Papa Bear defending the ones they love. You just have to remember it isn't worth fighting to defend your loved ones if in return someone else you truly love gets hurt in the process.

End of Story

Monkey Business

A SHORT STORY

As Fred walked past the palm tree, he heard Steve ask him sweetly, "how are you doing today", but instead of giving Steve a reply of "good morning, I'm doing fine and by the way how are you?" Fred just snapped back, "Why don't you just leave me alone and mind your own business?" Of course that offended Steve to the point that he never spoke to Fred again.

It seemed like everyone that tried to get close to Fred and carry on any kind of a conversation with him would always seem to get their feelings hurt when he would sharply end the conversation by reminding them that **his business** was none of their business. Fred never gave it even one more thought as he walked away from the other Monkeys that lived in his little grove of palm trees.

One day Fred decided to take a vacation to visit his brother. His brother lived only a few miles across the river, which was only just a day's journey from his home. Fred's brother really wasn't looking forward to his visit, but since Fred was his only brother, he put away his dread and opened his door to him. Once inside, it didn't take long before the conversation got around to what Fred had been up to since the last time they had met. Fred as usual, quickly shut his brother up and quickly reminded him that it was none of his business. Well as much as he wanted to visit with his brother, Fred had made his welcome turn into nothing but sour grapes for his brother, so Fred was asked to leave.

On his return trip from his brother's house Fred was chased off the trail by at least three wild dogs and before he knew it, he found himself lost and up a tree he had never seen before. It was dark before Fred was able to come back down from the tree's branches, and in the dark, Fred kept wandering off in the wrong direction.

On the third day of being lost in the jungle, Fred decided to stop walking and wait for someone to come and rescue him. He was sure once his brother and neighbors found out he was missing that they would all come looking for him. Then he remembered that he hadn't told anyone where he was going, so no one would even know in which direction to start looking for him. The words he said to his brother and friends kept ringing and ringing in his own ears, "that is none of your business – that is none of your business" over and over again until he knew he would have to get out of this predicament totally all by himself.

For as you see, if you decide to make "your business" totally out of anyone else's reach, then don't be surprised when they stop asking you questions and stop caring anything at all about "your business".

End of Story

Not In A Million Years

A SHORT STORY

Just look at how far man has advanced in just the 1/2 of a century that I have been alive. Who's to say where man will be in the next 1/2 of a century. I have to say it didn't happen over night, but just the same, it did happen.

One by one each lemming that went past the home of the next, would yell down into their neighbors' hole, "It's time to go, friend, its time to go." Then like clock work, the next lemming would do the same, until a massive migration of lemmings started marching off down to the sea.

Chip caught up with his friend Chuck at about the half way point in their journey. Chip was so excited to finally be going somewhere, other than their little patch of hillside, which he had to be told by Chuck to try and slow down and pace himself. Chuck said, "Chip if you tire yourself out now, then you won't be able to finish the swim we have to make over to the next island." Chip replied, "Thanks for reminding me, I'll slow down and we can both get to the cliffs together, but when we get there, I have a surprise to show you."

Chuck's eyes when opened wide with excitement as he said, "A surprise, you know how I love surprises."

Night fell and still the march continued. It wasn't until the dawn came that the water and cliffs could be seen off in the distance. About 20 feet from the cliff's edge, Chip stopped Chuck and told him it was now time to show him his surprise. Chip said, "Chuck haven't you ever wondered why we have so much extra skin under our armpits now a days, and why the older we get the more skin seems to grow there?" Chuck said, "Well, yeah, I have noticed, but my parents didn't have that much extra skin and you know as a matter of fact, my grandparents didn't have any extra skin at all, and so I just thought that maybe it was because I had put on a few extra pounds lately."

Chip chuckled as he looked under his arms, and pulled at the extra skin, then he told Chuck that his surprise would be finding out just exactly what their extra skin was going to be used for. Chip said, "Watch out cliffs, here I come." Then as he ran and leapt out from the cliffs edge he yelled, "Geronimo" Chuck was close on his heels, but stopped short of the edge as Chip spread out his arms and started gliding. The extra skin acted as if they were sails covering the wings of a glider, soaring him high in the air over the shoreline and then out to sea.

Chip circled back around and talked Chuck into giving his arms and his ability to fly, a running chance off the edge of the cliff. It didn't take long before the two of them were flying along on the wind currents with the rest of their friends getting their first flying lessons very close behind them.

For as you see, evolution has always been there to help make things on earth a little bit easier. So why does man always want to try and fight change? Just think about all the body parts you can live without today. They can remove your gallbladder, a kidney, a lung and your tonsils, as well as numerous limbs and reproductive organs. Also did you know that at one time or another in our evolutionary process, our appendix functioned and was a very necessary part of our existence, but even now it too has gone by the wayside and become something we can live without. So as the world takes on global warming it may become necessary for man to evolve one day, and grow fire resistant dragon like scales or maybe even deep-water gills just to survive what the future has in store for us.

End of Story

One Bad Apple

A SHORT STORY

At the edge of the clearing, just as the lights went on Jeff and Jerry sat and watched as this years Christmas Party was about to begin. Saddened by the fact that they wouldn't be invited to the party again this year the two of them just let out a long shy as the first present was handed out.

Jeff couldn't help but ask Jerry why he thought the people at the party couldn't understand that it wasn't them that had chased down the man and took a bite out of him. They had never done anything to harm anyone and as the Tigers that they are, a proud and well-mannered bunch, it would never cross their minds to do such a thing. Jeff asked, "Couldn't the Man tell by my short ears and crooked tail that it wasn't me that did all the biting?" Jerry replied, "No, once the damage is done, no Man will take the time or chance the risk that would be needed to determine one Tiger from another. **Once Fear is provoked, Fear will rule**."

Jeff had to agree with what Jerry had just told him, but he also had to add that now all the rest of the Tigers would have to suffer for what just one bad apple in the bunch had done. He said, "We ran that bad Tiger off a long time ago, but even though he is gone we still have to pay the price for all that he had done to men. How long will it take for the Man to forget, and let things get back to normal and the way it use to be?" Sadly Jerry whispered, "Man never forgets." Jeff added, "I sure would like a taste of those leftovers again. You know that was always the best part of the party. Oh well, I guess it will be no such luck again this year."

For as you see, one bad apple can spoil your taste for life and any chance for forgiveness, so try to not stereotype and group all apples into one bunch, because even if they are all apples, there will be sweet ones right along with the bitter, and good ones right next to the bad.

End of Story

See How Smart I Am

A SHORT STORY

Haven't you ever wondered how the Fox seems to always be able to out wit the Hound? Well there is a logical reason for that and it doesn't have anything to do with its physical differences, because if you put them side-by-side they are almost identical in stature. So the only advantage the Fox has over the Hound has to be located somewhere in its brain.

It became time to teach Ed's and Fred's sons the secret that all male Foxes learn once they come to Fox manhood. Ed started off by showing the young ones the den that he and Fred had built a good safe distance from their real homes. He showed them how it had a front door and then about ten feet away under a fallen tree trunk he showed them the back door to the den. Fred then took over and told the group how their usual workday started. Fred said, "Ed and I take turns keeping a watchful eye out for the Hound. He will usually not make any noise; that is until he locates us, and then he will bark continuously until he loses his voice and can't bark anymore. The

THE FOR AS YOU SEE TALES

little ones were all ears and tails and quickly absorbed ever word their Dad's had to say.

Off in the distance Ed caught the sound of the Hound as he came closer and closer to the den, so the guys hurried the kits (their sons) deep down into the den to keep them safe and sound as the chase began. Fred said, "Unless I'm wrong I think it is my turn to go first." Ed replied, "I think you are right, I think I went first yesterday." So Fred exited the den and went about 100 feet outside the opening. It wasn't long before Fred ran back into the den and tagged Ed on his backside, and that was when Ed took off running out the backdoor. One of the kits spoke up as he heard the barking of the Hound grow fainter and fainter. He said, "Dad I get it you and Ed play a game with the Hound kind of like when we play (tag you're it)."

Fred then told the group that is was more like running a relay race where you pass the baton from one runner to the next, only we keep passing the baton until the Hound can't run anymore. The only dangerous time is when the Hound is fresh and eager for the hunt. The Hound isn't smart enough to realize we are just taking him on a chase that makes a big circle back to this den, and that he is really chasing two different Foxes. He is so caught up in the thrill of the hunt that he can't think straight.

Jr. said, "what an ingenious plan. Who invented it?" Fred just said, "Son hold that thought, I'll be right back." It was then that Ed came in the front door and tagged Fred as he headed for the back door to tease the hound.

For as you see, survival really starts with being able to **"Out Wit" and then being able to "Out Last"**.

End of Story

The Real Reason The Dodo Bird Is Extinct

A SHORT STORY

Sure the Dodo bird was formerly found in Mauritius, Africa, but what you don't know is that it was originally from Australia. This is how the real story goes.

One day a most unlikely pair of Dodo Bird buddies went on a cruise. The second day at sea Sid turned and looked at Ralph, that was when he suddenly felt the need to comment on how all the other animals on board the ship seemed to have the same last name, because when the captain addressed them he would always say Mr. and Mrs. Tom Tiger or Mr. and Mrs. Mike Monkey. Sid then asked, "Ralph, when God commanded that you get on board this vessel and take this cruise what was his exact words?" Ralph had to think for a minute before he could answer Sid's question, but then when he remembered he said, "Let me see God told me that I needed to take a long trip and for me to go to Sidney and talk to a boat maker named Noah. Noah said that in a few days he would be setting sail for the open seas and he would be gone for 40 days and 40 nights. Why do you want to know? Aren't you having a great time with all of us on board this ship?"

Sid said, "Why of course I like the cruise and all the excitement, but I just can't get past the thought that maybe I shouldn't be the one to be here with you." Ralph added that he wouldn't have brought Sid with him if he didn't really enjoy his best friends' company. Ralph then spoke up and said, "Oh yeah, God told me just one more thing he said I would need to bring a "MATE" with me on this trip and you know Mate, that you are the best friend a man could have in the outback." Sid just sighed when he said, "Ralph, you have always been my best friend and a very good Mate to boot, and I'm really sorry to have to tell you this, but I think God had something else in mind for you, when he said for you to bring a "Mate" along with you on this boat ride. I think he meant for you to bring a "Sheila" as your "Mate". Ralph looked shocked when he said, "I guess I'll have to bring a Sheila along with me on my next boat trip."

For as you see, now you know why the Dodo Bird is really extinct. If God finds a need to command something of you; just make sure you fully understand all the fine details before you obey his command.

End of Story

Touché

A SHORT STORY

Did you know that when Swordfish are born their noses are no longer than our own? It is not until they reach the age of puberty that they are given the opportunity to challenge other swordfish of their same age group for the honored right to grow a sword.

Each year when the ocean waters warm, and the tide turns away from the shore the annual festival of the swordfish is celebrated. For one day and one day only all the young swordfish get to compete in a fencing match to prove to everyone their manhood, with of course the ultimate prize being a new nose. Steve and Stern had drawn really high numbers out of the seashell box of numbers, and so they knew it would be some time before it became their turn to spar with the others, but they also knew that the waiting and watching could give them an added edge by not having to go to their fencing matches completely blind sighted. Steve found the waiting for him to be the hardest, so as he stood still and flicked his tail from side to side against the current he turned to Stern and asked him if he remembered any helpful pointers that their fencing teacher had

THE FOR AS YOU SEE TALES

taught them. Stern thought for a moment then he replied, "Yes, I remember the most important rule of fencing is to put honor before self." Steve said, "Yeah, and the next one he said is for us to never cheat. Winners never cheat and cheaters never win. I am pretty sure that is how he put it. Well I plan on doing whatever it takes to become a man, and make our teacher proud of us." Stern said, "Yeah, me to."

There was only one fencing bout scheduled ahead of them, so while they were waiting the two boys looked over at the ring next to them that is when they saw another one of the boys in their class discretely cheating just so he could win. He was using every dirty trick in the book just so he could win his sword of a nose, but after he claimed himself the winner, his nose started to grow and grow and didn't stop until it grew so long that it drooped to the floor right in front of him as the crowd was watching. It was then that their fencing teacher Mr. Swift came up to Steve and Stern. He asked them if they were ready to show everyone what he had taught them about becoming a man.

Steve said, "Yes Sir, but would you mind telling us what has just happened to Larry's nose over there in the next ring. We saw him cheat and now he can't hold up his own nose. Please tell me that isn't what is going to happen to us?" Mr. Swift replied, "No boys, but I guess you can tell Larry didn't pay that much attention in class when I warned him about cheating. Now every time he swims around his nose is going to fly back and smack him right on top of his own head, just simply because when he cheated, he didn't use any integrity, and that just happens to be the most important ingredient for growing a sword of steel, so instead of having a nose as hard and strong as the others he now has one filled with jelly instead."

Steve and Stern were barely listening when their numbers were being called out, and so they almost missed their turn at the bout for manhood. Still each one them were able to grow noses worthy of the most honorable swordfish and with any luck they will pass that honor right on down to their own sons one day.

For as you see, now many criminals would there be in this world, if like Pinocchio, their noses grew out longer and longer with each crime they decide to make against God and/or mankind? My guess is not very many.

End of Story

Why Not Make It Fun?

A SHORT STORY

You could say that Jeff and Jerry were brothers, since they happened to have hatched in the same lake almost exactly at the same time. Once they got strong enough to make the journey then they both swam down stream and out into the Ocean just off the coast of Alaska.

Each year the spawning season for the Alaskan Salmon brings sports fishermen from all over the globe to the rivers and lakes of Alaska; just as the mature Salmon start trying to make their journey back up stream into the original waters of their birth. Thousands and thousands of the mature Salmon fight not only the rushing waters, birds, bears, but also the fishermen who patiently wait for the Salmon's struggle upstream to begin.

Jeff and Jerry were united, not by chance, but by nature, as they started swimming up the river with the rest of the Salmon. Both of them were full of energy and ready to take on the task, but as the up hill climb progressed and the rapids increased in intensity, their energy level started to dwindle. At one of the resting spots Jeff looked at Jerry and said, "Man, I am not sure I am going to make it to the lake before someone has to carry me up there." Jerry replied, "Brother, you know now much I love you, but it's just that I have to say man I am getting really tired myself, so carrying you on my back will be totally out of the question."

Then Jeff took a deep breath and jumped to the next level in the stream. Once Jerry had followed him and made the jump, Jeff said, "You know I almost didn't make that one." Jerry added, "I was wondering if I was going to make it too, but when I saw you do it, I knew I could make it, if I just tried a little bit harder.

It sure would be nice to get to the lake before night fall." Jeff laughed and told Jerry that the only way he would get there in time was if Jerry pushed him up the slopes of flowing water. Jerry thought for a moment, then he rushed over to Jeff and with a swish of his tail, he hit Jeff on his right side and said, "Tag, you are it" then he jumped up to the next level in the stream. After realizing what Jerry had just done to him, Jeff yelled, "No way man, you are not going to get away with that move that easily. Look out, here I come."

The chase didn't end until both of them had reached their spawning grounds and once they both got there, all bets were off and it was every fish for himself with Mother Nature at the helm steering their fate.

For as you see, the way to make a difficult job less of a chore for you to do is to make it into a game instead.

End of Story

Winter In The Cedars

A Short Story

On the side of a great mountain there is a grove of cedar trees. Each spring when the time comes for the trees to send their seeds out into the wind, the air will be filled with floating white seedpods. Some will fall into the spring water and be swept away down stream. Some will be blown far away and be carried off to the valley below. A few will not be as fortunate and they will be forced to try and make it through the coming winter still up on the mountainside not far from their parent trees. These less fortunate seeds hardly stand a chance of ever taking root up on the rocky mountainside.

Sadie was one of the older more established trees in the grove, and one day she started up a conversation with Ms. Woodpecker who had been using her for years now as a nesting place and home with which to raise her young. Sadie said, "Excuse me but can I bother you for a moment Ms. Woodpecker?" Ms. Woodpecker said, "of course I have a moment. What can I help you with Sadie?" Sadie replied, "I really need to ask you to do something for me and in turn it will help you and your brood in the near future." Ms. Woodpecker said, "I'll gladly help you if I can. What do I need to do?"

Sadie let out a deep sigh and then started telling Ms. Woodpecker that it has been years since she was able to make seed pods, and in turn it will only be a few more years before it becomes time for her to be at the end of her cycle of life. When that happens Sadie said she will end up falling to the ground and if she doesn't do something now there won't be any tree there to take her place on the mountainside. Sadie also pointed out that she no longer could produce the seed herself so Ms. Woodpecker would have to do that for her. Sadie said, "Ms. Woodpecker next time you go out and find seed to feed your young with; I just need for you to drop one of those seeds at my root base. Among my roots just make sure you cover the seed you place there with dirt and leaves. If you place it on the South downhill side of my roots I will be able to protect it from any snowfall or avalanches.

If you will do this then I will do the rest and when the time comes the seedling will be there for the both of us." Ms. Woodpecker flew away and squawked "What a good idea. It is as good as done." With the coming of spring came the first snowmelt and as the grass started to rise out of the ground so did the cedar sapling. As he straightened up to shake the dirt of his head and stretch out his arms just at her feet Sadie said, "Good morning little one. Happy birthday, I think I'll name you Sadie Jr. Are you ready to greet the new day?"

For as you see, every creature on earth will in one way or another affect the life of some other creature. Life is funny that way.

End of Story

A Dog's Tail

A SHORT STORY

It has been brought to my attention that maybe you do not know me. It seems a proper introduction is needed before this story can be told.

Hi my name is Boots and the dog sitting right next to me is my oldest brother Rover. Even though we look nothing alike and think nothing alike, we do come from the same litter of pups, so by all definitions of the word then, yes, brothers are what we are.

Our newly acquired next door neighbor's dog lives all alone with only his owner (Fred) and his owner's Son to come out and keep him company. Rover over heard Fred say one day, "Rex come here", which brought both the little boy and the dog back into the house, so Rover is still somewhat confused as to which one's name is truly Rex. Either way Rex is as good name as any in my opinion.

One day as we sat quietly watching our owner (Mike) cut the back yard grass we noticed Fred come walking over to the fence and start talking to Mike about all kinds of manly grass cutting stuff. They compared the horse power of their lawn mowers and how long it takes for each of them to get the job of cutting their grass done. Then the topic shifted to Rex and all the holes Rex had been digging in Fred's back yard. Fred complained about how he had to continually keep filling the holes back in each week before he could even start to get his grass cut.

That was when we both looked at each other, and then quickly we went over to the fence, because even though the two men didn't know what the problem with Rex was; Rover and I knew exactly what it would take in order to get Rex to stop digging up his owner's back yard.

Rover and I started waging our tails and sticking our noses through the fence. It only was a second or two before we got nose to nose with Rex through the fence. That was when we three started barking loudly while waging our tails. It wasn't long before both men stopped talking and looked down at us. Then almost like synchronized swimming; all three of us; Rover, Rex, and I sat down at the fence and just stared at each other. You could see the moment on our owner's faces when they finally realized what the problem was. It was almost as if they could read our minds; the same way they know exactly what we are begging for when we need a treat or two.

All of a sudden the gate opened up and Rex ran over and joined my brother and me in a big game of tug of war. Just so you know tug of war is better played with a crowd. The games went on for hours and hours, but guess what, not one single hole got dug while the three of us enjoyed each other's company. Now every time the men come out into their back yards it seems like the gate will open up and then it is game on. If you really want to know the truth, Rover and I do miss seeing Rex digging holes, but getting to play with Rex instead of watching him dig is so much more rewarding in my book.

For as you see, all problems have a solution, if you are just willing to try and get past them to figure the solution out. Company does love Company!

End of Story

CHAPTER TWO

FOR THE YOUNG AT HEART

A Story A Day Keeps The Doctor Away

A SHORT STORY

Jake was already tucked into his little car bed by the time his Dad came into his room to read him to sleep from one if his favorite books. As his Dad turned the bedside light on and walked over to the little bookcase, he softly asked Jake what book he wanted his bedtime story read from, since they had finished the one about the giant and the bear the night before, so Jake would have to pick another one for tonight's bedtime story. Jake said, "Read me the one about the dragon and the dragonfly, Daddy." His Dad said, "Ok" and then scanned the bookshelf in front of him until he came across the brightly colored book with a dragon and a castle on the cover page. His Dad said, "Here it is" then he sat down on the bed right beside Jake.

As always a good story starts out with (Once upon a time), then after reading him the first few words, his Dad asked if Jake needed a drink of water before he started to read him the rest of the story.

THE FOR AS YOU SEE TALES

Jake replied, "If you wouldn't mind Daddy, I sure am thirsty." His Dad always kept a fresh drink of water close by, as a lifeline just at bedtime. After getting a drink of water for Jake, his Dad sat back down beside him and started reading him the first story in the book, which was titled (The Dragon and The Dragonfly).

It was only after the first page that the story really got to the good parts, so baby Jake would always make sure he managed to stay awake at least until after the dragon met the dragonfly. You could tell by the smile on his face that Jake's Dad also really liked that part of the story his best part as well. His Dad never missed putting all the punctuation marks in his voice at just the right time, which would always make the stories just that much more magical. As the words, "Of course the dragonfly always defeated the dragon" came out of his mouth, his Dad softly turned out the light and kissed his little man a goodnight kiss, and then they both slept the night away with dreams of castles, knights, and of course chasing dragons.

For as you see, make time to read to your children, because stories are what dreams are made of.

End of Story

All The Kings Horses And All The Kings Men

A SHORT STORY

At the foot of the wall laying in a million pieces was the empty shell of Humpty Dumpty. All the Kings Men gathered around Humpty Dumpty and talked about who was going to clean up the mess that just cracking one egg had made. One of the men said, "I sure am glad it wasn't a whole dozen of eggs that fell off the wall." Another man said, "You know Humpty was the Kings favorite egg, I wonder who is going to inform the King of his favorite egg's demise."

Just then the Captain of the Guard came upon the scene and brought his men to attention. As they all lined up his first question was, "who pushed Humpty off the wall?" All the men got quite. So the Captain repeated the question and added that he knew someone had to have seen what had just happened to Humpty and before any of them could go about their business of the day, he would have to have some answers. One of the men spoke up and said, "No one pushed Humpty off the wall he just lost his balance and since his

THE FOR AS YOU SEE TALES

arms were so short he couldn't hold on long enough for us to get to him, and so he fell. It was totally an accident." The Captain told them that he believed him, but that wasn't going to make the King any happier and would someone like to volunteer to go and tell the King the bad news. No one spoke up so the Captain knew he would have to be the one who approached the King with the bad new of the day.

A couple of days past before word got back to the men that there Captain had been thrown into the King's dungeon. The very next day the Captain's job vacancy was posted on the Human Resources Bulletin Board.

For as you see, I never have been anyone's boss and there is a good reason for that. I have seen bosses come and I've seen bosses go, but guess what **I'm still here**.

End of Story

And This Too Shall Pass

A SHORT STORY

The thought of summer vacation, for a child of Timmy's age, was all he ever dreamed of each summer that rolled around. Once school let out and the days got warmer his parents had promised to take him down to the coast of Florida to play for a couple of days. Timmy had never seen a beach or felt the waves rush past his feet as they washed ashore. The only thing he knew of the Atlantic Ocean was what he had seen on TV or read about in a magazine; mostly what he knew of the Ocean was that it was very big and salty.

The car was packed the night before they left and each child picked their seat by the window except for Timmy, of course, since he was the youngest he always was picked to get stuck in the middle of the back seat. His Sister sitting to his right brought her favorite book to read and his Sister sitting on his left brought her earphones and favorite music to listen too. Timmy brought his games to keep him busy, but since his attention span was relatively a short one, the games he brought didn't last him past the first day's drive out on the road. Timmy's parents had already explained to him that the trip would be a very long one, so depending on how far their Dad could drive the first day and/or how good the driving weather was on the trip; these factors combined would decide when they would be able to get there.

Even knowing how far away the water was and even knowing about how many days travel it would be, that didn't stop Timmy from asking the predictable questions of, "how much farther is it and how long will it take now." His parents always reassured him by saying; "it won't be long now, baby" which would buy them about an hour before he couldn't stand it any longer and the questions would then repeat themselves.

It was after dark when the family car rolled to a stop in the driveway of the condo they had rented just adjacent to the beachfront. Of course the first thing out of Timmy's mouth was "are we there yet", as they woke him up to get him out of the car and with a great sign of relief his Mother replied, "Why yes baby we are."

Timmy was too sleepy to get very excited at that point in time; it took all he had just to jump into bed for the rest of the night. The next morning his eyes popped wide open and his little feet hit the floor a running as he opened the front door. Instead of seeing the bright sun shinning down on a sandy shore, all the little boy saw was dark clouds and rain drops. He asked his Mom, "why is it raining and when will it let up?"

His Mom stopped cooking just long enough to tell him that when they had planned their trip that they had no way of knowing what the weather might be at that time and then she told him that she was sorry but the weather man said it might rain the whole time they were there. Timmy's mouth flew open and you could tell that at any moment he would start to cry. All his Mom could do was stop and tell him that if he wanted to wait until after breakfast that she would sit down and play a game with him; even though that didn't lessen his disappointment it did seem to dry his eyes.

The day drug on and the night was even longer and for two days straight it rained. Timmy's hopes of playing on the beach ebbed in and out almost as often as the water with the tide constantly washing up on its shore. There was only one day left with only one more chance for Timmy to get to make the sand castle of his dreams. He was slow to get out of bed, almost dreading to open the curtain to his bedroom window, he knew, he just knew it would still be raining, but instead this last day brought the joy of glorious sunshine. I have never seen a child get dressed in a bathing suit quite that fast, is what his Mom told his Dad as they sat in their lawn chairs drinking their morning coffee watching shovels of sand go flying around in piles at their feet.

For as you see, one day it rained for 40 days and 40 nights with everything in sight seeming all dank and gloomy, but as you know, when it eventually did stop raining the sun gloriously shone through. Even more so now, as it was then, the words "And This Too Shall Pass" hold true, you just need to be strong enough to wait out the storm.

End of Story

Musical Chairs

A SHORT STORY

As with most offices, this one is filled with groups of employees. Groups gravitate to people who share common interests. There was the water cooler group of those "over 50 years of age"; there was the outside group of "smokers", and then the 20 to 30 year old "video gamers". Each group got along with the other as long as they stayed in their own little cubicles.

Sometimes the group members had to communicate with each other while trying to hide their phones, and text messages from sight of their bosses. Personal communication was only to be done at scheduled breaks or lunch time. Of course the younger group members pulled off the phone text messaging while at work ploy the best without bringing any attention to the fact that they were texting while working on company time.

The company was a great place to work for. Each summer the company threw all their employees a company bar-b-que picnic, and for each holiday the office put up multiple decorations in celebration of another successful year in the black profit line instead of in the red.

Christmas parties were the best, and this year it was decided that one of the games played would be musical chairs. The game was set up with one chair in the middle of the room with the tables set up in a circle around it. Each group got to pick four players and there were five groups. The over 50's, the 20 to 30's, the smokers, and last but not least there was the management group playing against each other. Each time the music stopped another player was sent to their table just to sit and watch the music start and stop over and over again.

One by one the players were eliminated, at first the company crowd were all smiles and laughing, but by the time it got to the last four players remaining, you could see and feel the change of fun level atmosphere all around the room.

When it came down to the last two fighting for chair dominance, everyone was holding their breath. Would the younger group win or would the last chair go to management? The music began. Round and round they went as the two of them circled the chair. Then the music stopped and the winner got the chair and the loser got to go to the hospital with a broken arm.

For as you see, what starts out as fun and games can quickly end in a disaster. Spending your Christmas bonus on doctor bills will definitely take the fun out of "fun and games". Playing nicely is the best way to play. If someone gets hurt then nobody wins.

End of Story

Cause And Effect

A SHORT STORY

Tim was having a good old time of flicking the light switch on and off when his Dad opened the door. His Dad said, "Son, I thought your Mom told you to go to bed hours ago." Tim lowered his head and replied, "Yes Daddy she did, but I can't understand why my light goes out when I flick this switch down and then comes back on when I flick it up." His Dad then had to explain to Tim all about electricity until both of them were too tired to continue, so his Dad put him to sleep and said that they would discuss it more in the morning.

The next day bright and early Tim went into his Dad's bedroom and started flicking his Dad's light switch on and off until it woke both of his parents up and made the light bulb burn out. Instead of getting angry with his little boy, Tim's Dad just started trying to tell him about why the light bulb had burned out and why his electricity bill was going to go out of the roof if Tim continued to turn the light switch on and off all the time. His Dad said, "That is what we call (Cause and Effect) the light bulb only has a set number of hours it will burn and then it will burn itself out. So if you keep turning it on and off you will just be wasting the light bulb." Tim said, "Ok Daddy I understand why you do not want me to flick my switch anymore so I promise I won't."

Years past, and Tim was fastly becoming a teenager. His Dad started seeing his Son go through all the growing pains that comes with growing up and knew it was time to have another "man to man" talk with him. They both sat down at the kitchen table and started talking. Tim went first and said, "Dad if this is a talk about the birds and the bees", but before Tim could say another word his Dad intervened by saying, "No Son this talk is about turning the lights on and off." Tim looked puzzled when he questioned his Dad as to what he was trying to say to him. His Dad just said, "Son you are at the age where you will start pushing your body to its limits. You will stay up late, do extreme sports, date girls, and maybe even try drugs and alcohol."

Tim quickly replied, "no, not me Dad." His Dad said, "I sure hope you don't, but if you do, I also hope you will think it over before you put your body through something you will live to regret later on in your life. Promise me you will try and remember just one think I am going to tell you today, all I ask is that you remember your body is just like that light bulb." His Dad then pointed to the ceiling, and said, "you can use your body properly or you can abuse it, and just like that light bulb, your one and only body, the one God has given to you, has a limited number of times that you can abuse it before, just like that light bulb, the abuse will make parts of your body finally quit working properly for you."

His Dad finished by telling him that it will maybe fun to take his body to its extreme limits, but that fun will also go away the very next day, where the damage it does to his body will be with him forever. Tim stopped his Dad there and told him that he promised to remember the light bulb, anytime he was tempted to abuse anything, **especially himself**.

For as you see, the abuse you put your body through today is something you will have to deal with and medically treat tomorrow.

End of Story

Is It Contagious?

A SHORT STORY

The sign reads, "CAUTION <u>hypergraphia</u> is at work here".

After signing in at the front desk the two elderly Sisters sat down at the back of the room while waiting their turns to see the Doctor. It wasn't long before the waiting room became so crowded that it was just standing room only, so to pass the time away the two Sisters whispered back and forth to each other. At first it was just their usual gossip about friends they both knew, but when that topic was covered completely they decided to try and guess what had brought all the other people around them into the office to see the Doctor.

Helen went first and said, "Sis, see the man sitting directly to my left." Judy said, "Sure do and the way he is sitting in that chair I bet he is here with back pain." Helen said, "Good guess, but if you look a little bit closer at the way he is squirming you will see that he probably has a problem with his hemorrhoids." Judy replied, "you know you are could be right, but if I had my choice between the two problems, I surely would pick having back pain over the other any day of the week."

After a couple more good guesses the patients became harder and harder for the two of them to diagnosis, until there was only one little girl left undiagnosed in the room. Judy told Helen that she really couldn't figure out why a young healthy little girl like that one, would ever have to come in to see their Doctor. Helen just laughed and then replied, "Sis, just look at her a little bit harder, can't you see that she has hypergraphia?" Judy said, "No, I can't, but do you think that <u>hypergraphia</u> is contagious?" Helen then busted out laughing at Judy when she told her; "I know you can see it from here, because hypergraphia is **written** all over her face. I also think that if you really want to know whether or not it is contagious, then you will just have to go over and ask her Mother, but definitely make sure you hold your breath the whole time you are over there, because you never know when it might be catching."

For as you see, not all disease processes are bad ones, take getting older for example, exactly where do you think you would be, without that one working on you daily? So even if I have hypergraphia, it wouldn't be such a bad thing, considering you are reading this story, and I am sitting here with this really big grin on my face dreaming of what the next story I'm writing might be. Case closed or should I say–

End of Story

Lullaby

A SHORT STORY

There is an Irish Lullaby that my Mother sang to me when I was a little baby. That song holds the very first memory I have of my Mother, and the words she sang to me each night were warmer than any woolen blanket or softer than the most beautiful nightingale's song. All the other stories in the world can't do this one justice, so hold on tight.

Nothing you could offer as a bribe could get little Joey to go to bed that night. Helen, his baby sitter, had trying everything she could think of to get this little boy to go to bed. Helen had been pushed to her limit before she finally picked up the phone and called Joey's Mom. After she explained her dilemma his Mom then asked her to put Joey on the phone so she could talk to him. All Helen could hear was Joey saying, "Yes Momma, yes Momma, but when are you coming home?" then Joey gave the phone back to Helen and when back to playing with his ball. Before hanging up the phone Helen got his Mom's permission to let him stay up really late until she could return home from her meeting.

Joey could hear the car door shut and his Mom's footsteps as she walked towards the front door. So he ran and jumped into her arms the moment she walked in the door, even before she could set her purse down. Helen was paid for her babysitting time and after she had left for home, Joey and his Mom closed and locked the house up for the night. Joey never left his Momma's right hip and it didn't take anytime before his little head was resting on her shoulder with his fist all balled up and rubbing his eyes.

His bed was fixed and ready for him by the time she got him to bed, so after he climbed in between the sheets his Mom asked, "Baby do you want me to read you a story or do you want Momma to sing you to sleep." Joey said, "Sing to me Mommy." His Mom sat down on the bed and tucked him in, kissed him on his forehead and started to sing, "Too-ra-loo-ra-loo-ra, Too-ra-loo-ra-li, Too-ra-loo-ra-loo-ra, hush now, don't you cry!"

Joey started yawning and his little eyes were shut when his Mom continued singing, "Over in Killarney many years ago, my Mother sang this song to me in a voice so soft and low. Just a simple Irish ditty, in her good old Irish way, and I'd give the world if she could sing that song to me this day." By that time her voice had hushed to just a whisper and she leaned over and kissed her baby boy goodnight one more time, before she went off to her bed.

For as you see, nothing on this earth can take the place of your Mother's sweet goodnight. It doesn't matter whether it is by song or story, it is all still her **LOVE**.

End of Story

Not So Close

A SHORT STORY

When you are the oldest in a family of four children, nothing will get your attention any quicker than the sound of your youngest brother crying. So even with Sarah's radio turned up blaring out the latest teen idle hit music, she sat straight up and turned the volume knob down really low and then completely off, as she listen for what she knew was crying coming from down the hallway in the direction of Robert's room. As he softly lay crying in his bed, Robert first heard Sarah knock then crack open the door and stick her head in just to check up on him. Robert invited her in and then he quickly wiped away his tears on his bed sheets just before she came near enough to notice. Robert having just turned 10 was way too old to let his almost grown up 16 yr old Sister see him cry, so even with no evidence of tears on his face she still knew something was wrong.

Sarah sat down on his bed and asked him how his day at school had gone and did he need any help with anything like maybe his homework. Robert knew that Sarah was good at almost all school projects, but never to ask her to help with any math problems unless he wanted a few more problems than just math to deal with. Sarah had really good common sense, but a math wizard she definitely was not. It took a minute or two for Robert to loosen up and let Sarah know what was troubling him, but as soon as he did it was like a heavy weight had been lifted up off his shoulders. It all boiled down to his science project. Simply enough, it consisted of documenting a day in the life of a fish. Every 5 minutes Robert needed to be writing down just exactly what his two guppies were doing for the whole afternoon that day up until time for him to go to bed. Robert showed Sarah the information he had collected so far and for the last two hours every 5 minutes had "no fish in sight" written down in the lines beside it.

Sarah asked her little brother if that was what had him so upset and worried, and Robert said, "Yes, how am I going to turn in my report if I can't even see the fish." Sarah laughed, and then asked Robert to show her how he was going about doing his observations.

Robert waited until one of the fish came out from behind its shell home and then he walked over to the glass aquarium with his magnifying glass in his hand. As he leaned down to watch the fish all of a sudden it ran back into its shell home.

Robert said, "see Sister, it runs away from me and I do not know why." Sarah said, "Brother hand me that magnifying glass and tell me what you see". Robert watched as Sarah raised the magnifying glass up to her eye and that was when he saw just how big it actually made her eye look. Robert said, "Whoa, Sis you really look scary with that one big eye. I don't think I would even want to come near you". Sarah replied, "Now you see what the fish sees. Let me show you what you need to do." Sarah sat Robert down on the edge of his bed and they both sat there and waited until the fish came back out of their shell home. Sarah told Robert to just wait there for a moment then she left the room, upon her returning she handed him a pair of binoculars, and said, "See, now you can observe them and they won't mind it so much". Robert finished his science project, the fish were a lot happier and they both received an (A) for effort on a job well done.

THE FOR AS YOU SEE TALES

For as you see, constant scrutiny promotes mutiny. No one can do a good job if they are questioned with every move they make. Questions like "Did you do this or did you do that?" asked over and over again will make even the most loyal person want to jump ship.

End of Story

Planting A Seed

A SHORT STORY

George's garden on average would be considered a small one, but to him it was all he could handle and still get the rest of his work done. One day as he was working his garden his youngest son, Greg, came out the back door and over to the garden to see what his Dad was up to and to tell him that supper would soon be ready for them to eat. George was so contently hoeing away at the plants that he was somewhat shaken to see Greg just a few feet away from him when Greg said, "Dad". After the initial shock wore off George said, "Hi Son, what do you need?" Greg was looking at the ground when he said, "Dad, Mom said that supper will be on the table shortly and for you to round up whatever you are doing and come on back inside."

George stopped hoeing just long enough to tell Greg that he would be there just as soon as he finished weeding out the rest of the row he was working on, and then he contently went back to hoeing. Greg took a few steps then he turned and questioned his Dad by asking him why he even had to hoe the garden at all. His Dad just laughed and said, "Son, when I spread the seed not all of the seed in the bag was seed that I wanted to plant, some of it would only grow weeds." Greg said, "but Dad can't you tell by looking at the seed which ones will not be what you want to grow?" His Dad replied, "No it isn't that easy to cull out the bad seed from the good, so once it starts to grow you have to take the hoe to the weeds and remove them before they take good root and ruin the good seed you have planted. Weeds grow fast and take all the food and sunshine away from everything that grows around them."

George then told Greg that it is kind of like when he meets a new friend, at school at first it is almost impossible to determine if they will be a good friend or end up being a bad one. He said, "Once you see the true character that will start to show in a friend then you will see the good or bad start to shine through, and then just like my hoeing the garden you will have to remove the bad friend before they start to take a good hold on your life."

Greg then said, "Dad you are right, and if I find a weed in my garden then I promise to take a hoe and remove it. OK!" His Dad said, "Great Son how lets go in for supper before your Mom takes her hoe to me." As they were walking to the door Greg asked his Dad just one more question he said, "Dad, how do you know that I won't turn out to be a bad seed?" George replied, "Well, Son that is an easy one to answer. I know you will grow up to be a very good Son, because I am the one who planted you and I made sure I planted you on <u>weed less ground</u>."

For as you see, it all started way back with another famous garden, the Garden Of Eden, and if you want to make sure your kids grow up to be good ones, then you had better start teaching them early about the Garden Of Eden, and then continue teaching them every week thereafter, because that is the best way to remove most of the weeds from their lives.

End of Story

For Patty and Paw Paw

That's Not What I Wanted

A SHORT STORY

Some of my best Christmas memories started with finding my stocking Christmas morning. It would be full to the brim and over flowing with nuts, fruit, and then nickel and dime store trinkets. Nothing that would cost more than just a few dollars, because that is all my single Mom could afford, but which was totally priceless to me. Thank you Santa (AKA Mom).

By the way, when you cut your Christmas oranges in half they will make a really big bad stain on the wall it lands on. One that won't come off newly painted sheet rock walls when you throw one of them at your little brother. Believe me, I know this from personal experience, and then of course all a little kid like me could do to try and cover up the stain was to color a picture on a piece of paper and then tape it over the Orange stained wall. Then when she asks who the pictures on the wall are for; you can just tell her they were colored just especially for her then smile a big smile.

Larry and Wendy were sitting at their kitchen table trying to make out their Christmas list for their two little boys went their

THE FOR AS YOU SEE TALES

youngest son Mike came in the back door. Wendy said, "baby, come over here and tell Mommy and Daddy what you want Santa to bring you for Christmas this year. Have you made out a wish list for me to mail to Santa at the North Pole?" Mike said, "I sure have Mommy, I'll go and get it for you." It wasn't but a minute before he came back with a very short list of wishes that he wanted Santa to bring him. Wendy then asked Mike if he would go and find his Brother Ken because he also needed to bring his wish list to her so she could mail both of their lists to Santa at the same time.

It wasn't long before Ken ran down the stairs and handed his wish list to his Mom. Wendy took one look at the three pages of things he wanted from Santa and said, "Ken, sweetie you know there is no way Santa can bring you all the things you have put on this list." Ken looked at her with a puzzled look on his face and said, "But, why not Momma? Santa can do anything and I want everything on the list. Santa knows how good I have been this year."

His Mom couldn't help but agree on how good he had been most of the year, and then she gave him a big hug. Ken's Dad said, "But Son, even if Santa's Elves worked overtime and got a really good Christmas bonus that won't even begin to touch all the expensive presents you have put on your list." Ken stopped as he was headed out the back door to finish playing and looked at his Mom and Dad and then said, "Mom, write Santa and tell him if he needs an extra Elf this year to help with my list then I will gladly help him, if you and Dad will let me, that is."

After Ken went back to playing Wendy looked at Larry and said, "I feel really sorry for poor Santa this year because he is going to have to work some really long hours just to try and fill Ken's wish list." Larry chuckled a little then added, "Yeah and I fell really sorry for poor Mrs. Clause, when it comes time for her to write a letter back to Ken, and try to explain to Ken the reasons why Santa just couldn't make all that he had asked for this year squeeze down very small little chimney at our house."

For as you see, it would be really nice to have all that you wish for each year from Santa, but when you can't, then you should always try and remember as many of the past wonderful Christmas Holidays you have had, the ones where your Mom (AKA Santa) was around to enjoy them with you.

End of Story

The Bully

A SHORT STORY

Toby always looked up to his Uncle Mike. Uncle Mike taught him how to swim and ride his first bike also he stood up for him when he needed someone to. So Uncle Mike was the first one Toby turned to when the school bully started harassing him for his lunch money every morning before school started. The first couple of times that Toby came home and headed straight for the refrigerator looking for something to eat after school, Uncle Mike didn't pay that much attention to it, but when it became an everyday thing of coming home from school hungry, his Uncle Mike started taking notice.

The bullying rocked on for about a week before Uncle Mike decided to take some action. One morning as the bully had Toby pinned to the ground demanding his lunch money and refusing to not let him up until he said out loud "Uncle", the bully got more than what he bargained for? Just as Toby started to say "UNCLE", he hesitated for a moment then he said – "UNCLE, Uncle Mike I thought you would never get here." The bully looked over his right shoulder and when he saw this very large man standing really close to him; he jumped up and started to take off running, but before he could, Uncle Mike stopped him right in his tracks. Uncle Mike knelt down and told the bully that now it was going to be his turn to say UNCLE, and for the bully to turn his head towards the tree just so he could talk directly into the video camera that was set up next to it. Uncle Mike then told the bully to repeat what he was about to say to him; he told him to repeat after me "Uncle Mike, if you ever catch me bullying any other little boys or girls around the school yard then next time it will cost me and my parents a whole lot more than just my lunch money.

If I decide to continue being a bully, you have what I just did on video tape and can and will use it against me in the near future if you ever find a need to do so, OK." Then Uncle Mike just said, "Remember little bully, someone is always seeing what you are doing anytime you might decide to be mean."

For as you see, the only way to stop a bully is to let them know that it is a crime they won't be able to get away with. Big Brother is always watching. Being caught on camera has put away a lot of bad people. DNA has freed a lot of innocent people as well.

End of Story

The Dragon And The Dragonfly

A SHORT STORY

This is not your usual David and Goliath story, although the outcome is basically the same.

The seats around the arena were full to the bream, so if you just happened to be fashionably late as Bud and Bill were today, then you had no other choice but to stand and watch the tournament from ground level until a few seats were to come open in the bleachers. It wasn't the first time the two of them were so unfortunate by being so late that they had to just stand around.

The trumpet sounded the end of the jousting match. It was at that time that most of the people who had come just to see the winner of the jousting contest, decided to get up and leave. Bud and Bill saw their golden opportunity to get a seat, but just as they were about to move into the open chairs they saw a Mother and child standing next to them waiting for a seat also. Just like the gallant gentlemen that they are, they let them have their seats and they waited until some more would come open.

While they were waiting Bud asked Bill which dragon did he think would be the winner of the first round of the "Battle of the Dragons" contest. Of course Bill picked the favorite to come in as the winner and Bud picked the underdog. The favorite and Bill's pick won the first round with little to no effort on the dragons' part. Bill was so proud of himself that he decided to start making the contest a little bit more interesting by making a betting wager of 5 shillings with his friend that he could predict the winner of each round. Bud didn't have anything else to do, so he told his friend that the bet was on.

Bill's dragon picks had won him about 10 rounds when the last contest was about to begin. Bud was smiling when he found out that the last battle would be one between a dragon and a dragonfly, so when his friend Bill said he was going to bet on the dragon, Bud quickly took the bet and told him that the dragonfly was going to win this battle and he was so sure the dragonfly would win that he wanted to increase his bet to 500 shillings.

Since it was the last battle of the day and he was so positive a dragonfly had absolutely no chance of winning any battle with a dragon, Bill gladly accepted Bud's bet of 500 shillings.

It is a good thing that a couple of seats became open for the last battle, because what happened next would have taken the legs right out from under Bill if he had of been standing. Right out of the gate the dragon headed for the little box that housed the dragonfly, but before the dragon could get close enough to burn the box with his breath, the dragonfly took to flight. The first place the dragonfly lighted upon was right between the dragon's ears on top of the dragon's head. The dragon's arms weren't long enough to reach the dragonfly, and though he shook and shook his head until it made him angry and dizzy, the dragonfly didn't budge.

Next the dragon decided to use his tail to squash the dragonfly, so with a mighty flail of his tail, the dragon hit himself right on top of his own head. Of course the dragonfly had moved at just the right time and watched as the dragon let out a roar, then the dragonfly landed on the dragon's back out of reach of the dragon's hand or

THE FOR AS YOU SEE TALES

tail. The dragon was at a disadvantage, he knew the only way to get the dragonfly off his back was to blow his fiery breath at his own backside, and with his head still hurting from the blow from his own tail, the dragon wasn't in any hurry to singe his own backside with his own breath. So the dragon took flight to try and shake the dragonfly off, but the faster the dragon flew, the more the dragonfly held tight. It wasn't long before the dragon tired out to the point that he couldn't even hold his head up when he landed in the arena. As the dragon lay on the ground with his eyes closed and nothing but smoke coming from his nostrils, the dragonfly gently landed back on top of the dragon's head. That was when the contest was over and the dragonfly was announced the winner, and of course the two friends never wanted to bet against each other again.

For as you see, the dragonfly actually didn't beat the dragon. The dragon was defeated and weakened to the point of exhaustion, by something as small and simple as his own frustrations and rage.

End of Story

For Jason

The Five Second Rule

A SHORT STORY

Jim and Steven were old enough to be left in the back yard unsupervised, but still young enough to require Jim's Mom to check in on them from her kitchen window at fairly regularly timed intervals. Jim's Mom would always send him out to play with a morning snack in his hand and of course a few more snacks bagged up just to share with any of his friends that might venture over to play with him.

It wasn't long before Jim came back inside to get his Mom to wash off his sucker that he had just dropped on the concrete. His Mom washed it off really good and then handed it back to him. As Jim turned to go back outside to play he stopped for a minute and then asked his Mom why it wasn't gross for her to just wash off his sucker instead of making him throw it away like Steven's Mom makes him do. His Mom just chuckled and said, "Baby, there is what I like to call "the five second rule". If something can be cleaned off after it falls to the floor then it would be such a waste to just throw it away." Jim replied, "Mom, you are right it's just that

Steven's Mom makes such a fuss with him for something she calls germs. She makes him throw a lot of good things away." His Mom chuckled again and told him that there are germs all around him, all the time and to try and keep him from getting any germs would mean that she would have to place him in a bubble where nothing could ever touch him. She then told him to go back to playing and if he dropped another sucker then just bring it back to her before he put it back into his mouth. He assured her that he would, then out the door he went.

It wasn't long before Steven brought his sucker into the house for Jim's Mom to wash off, but since Steven's Mom was so picky about not letting him have something that had hit the ground; she told him that he had better just throw that one away and get another sucker from Jim. Steven went back outside to play, and when the time came for the boys to come back inside Jim's Mom stopped in her tracks.

Then she started laughing when she saw the two boys sitting next to each other steadily passing a sucker from one of them to the other, each one taking a long slow lick off it before handing it back to the other one. Jim's Mom was still grinning when she told the boys it was time to go, but before she said goodbye to Steven she just had to ask him why he was sharing his sucker with Jim. Steven's answer was very simple, he just said, "Because it was the last one, Miss Jones."

For as you see, All the efforts you take to try and make your world germ free goes right out the window, the second your child enters the room.

End of Story

The Story Teller

A SHORT STORY

John was sitting at his kitchen table drinking his morning coffee when his friend Jacob came over to join him. As usual John had an ink pen in his hand and an open notebook in front of him. Since the notebook was only open to the first couple of pages Jacob could tell at a quick glance that John was on his way to writing another great book. Jacob sat down at the table and started drinking the cup of coffee that he had just poured for himself, that's when he started the conversation off by asking, "John, have you finished your last book, and have you picked out a title for this new one yet?" John answered Jacob by saying, "yes, I read the ending of my last book to the baby last night and now I am off to writing my next book. I really don't think I'll name this one just yet, I think I'll wait for a few more chapters before I decide what the title to this one will be."

Jacob sat for a minute then he just had to ask John why he would want to read his stories to his new born baby every night, especially since his new born son couldn't understand a word that he was saying to him. John just let out a chuckle, and said that he reads to the baby, because reading out loud helps him concentrate on what he is going to put into the next chapter of the story he will be writing the next day. John explained that most of what he writes comes from the dreams he has had the night before, and reading out loud helped him guide his dreams in the right direction. John then added that sometimes his stories come from his **day**dreams also, but either way it was still dreaming day or night that helped him write his stories.

Jacob took another drink of his coffee and then asked John if there was anyway he could help him with the book. John said, "You sure can, I would love to read the first few lines of my book out loud to you and see what you think of it." Jacob stopped drinking, put his cup down, and started listening as John told him, "it is going to be a book filled with Elves, Dwarfs, and let's see, oh yeah, a Ring."

For as you see, a Good Book was once a really Good Story, and there aren't any Movies made today that weren't first a very Good Dream.

End of Story

There Is A Snake In Our House

A SHORT STORY

John always woke up before his wife Helen in the mornings, so he would sweetly get up and go downstairs to start the morning coffee to percolating. After that he would come back upstairs to wake up Helen and their son Tim. This morning as John sat down on the bed to give Helen her good morning wake up kiss he also told her he had some bad news that he thought she should know before she went down stairs to make her usual bacon and egg breakfast for her crew.

Helen sat straight up and started asking John a bombardment of questions. John said, "Helen, slow down. The problem we have is that there is a snake in the house." Helen took a deep breath and then asked, "John, how do you know there is a snake in here?" John started by telling her to think back to when Tim had brought home about 10 frogs for his first school science project and how before he had finished his homework that all the frogs he had remaining was 5 out of the 10 frogs he had started with. He said, "Remember we thought that 5 of them had just gotten out one by one, well now I know better." Then he continued by asking her if she remembered

THE FOR AS YOU SEE TALES

his second science project the one where Tim had to raise a family of mice. Helen started shaking when she remembered that the mice also seemed to miraculously get out of their cages and disappear one at a time over a time span of several months. Then she said, "We just simply thought Tim was to blame for having let them out of their cages." John said, "Yes, I remember and how I know that it wasn't his fault at all for their vanishing act."

Helen then said, "OK John, how I need to know just how you are so sure that there is a snake in our house." John took her by the hand and walked her down the stairs to their living room. Helen told him that if he was going to show her a snake then he had better clear her a path because she was going to exit the house. John said, "Baby, you know I wouldn't do that to you. What I have to show you is right here." It was at that moment that he lifted the cover off her birdcage.

Helen instantly understood why John was so positive about the snake, because instead of her pretty yellow parakeet sitting on his perch where she had left him the night before, all that remained was yellow feathers. She immediately asked John if he could tell if the snake was a poisonous one or not. John replied, "What difference would it make, none of us want to have a snake in our house, whether it is a harmless one or not, it is still a snake." Helen said, "That is a point well taken" as she slowly bent over to look under her chair.

For as you see, you do not have to find the snake just to know that one has been in your house, and the only way to ever rid yourself of it is to catch it in a trap, otherwise you will always be expecting it to come back and strike at you again at any time it chooses.

End of Story

There Is A Storm Coming

A SHORT STORY

Fred's Grandpa rubbed his left arm and then looked down at Fred who was walking right beside him. Fred was having to walk pretty fast to try and keep up with his Grandpa so when his Grandpa came to a sudden stop, Fred was about two steps ahead of him before he could stop walking. Fred turned and asked his Grandpa, "Why have we stopped?" His Grandpa replied, "I feel a storm coming, because my left arm is staring to hurt." Fred started to panic because he knew it could also be a sign of something much more serious about to happen.

The look on Fred's face let his Granddad know exactly how concerned Fred was starting to get, and so to put Fred's mind to ease his Grandpa said, "Fred, let me tell you a little story about the fish and the crow." Fred's Granddad found a fallen tree trunk for them to sit on and that was when the story began.

Grandson there once was a Crow who would always go to the same pond to get a drink of water; at about the same time of each day. You could almost set your watch by the Crow's daily visit to

THE FOR AS YOU SEE TALES

the pond, so it was of no wonder that all the fish along the shore took note of the Crow's daily activity. Seasons would come and seasons would go, but it would take only the worst of bad weather to keep the Crow away from the pond and keep him at his roost to go thirsty until the weather changed. One day the Crow didn't show at his usual time so one of the fish said out loud, "it must really be bad weather up there, bad enough to keep the Crow from coming today." One of the other fish replied, "It might be bad weather up there, but how does that concern you since our weather down here never changes?" The first fish answered by saying, "bad weather doesn't really concern us, but it is just that when the weather gets bad enough to keep the Crow away, I can't help but feel sorry for the Crow."

After finishing the story Fred said, "Good story Grandpa, but just what did it have to do with your arm hurting?" Grandpa replied, "Well I'm just like that old Crow, I can tell by the way my old arm hurts as to whether or not the weather will be bright and sunshiny or dull and gray. My arm hurts from arthritis, and it will always hurt me at the first sign of bad weather. So don't concern yourself with ever ache and pain your Grandpa has, because getting older brings on quite a few aches and pains of its own. OK." Fred said, "Thanks for the story and the advice Grandpa, I'll try not to worry about you and your arm so much. Now where were we going from here?" Grandpa just laughed and said, "We are headed down to the pond so we can sit and watch the Crows try to get a drink of water just before that storm I'm feeling gets here."

For as you see, anticipating <u>the worse</u> will usually send <u>the worse</u> a written invitation to your party.

End of Story

Tis The Season

A CHRISTMAS POEM

What kind of Christmas would it be without a Christmas Story?
I know, I know, it would be a Christmas without Christ's Glory.
Well I am here to tell you, without further ado,
I have a Christmas story just for you.
In Louisiana, Christmas's come and Christmas's go,
I just wish for once it would come and bring us some snow.
Some say Santa down South has a sled,
that is drawn not with Reindeer, but with Gators instead.
How odd that would be,
if when you looked you would see,
not antlers or hoofs, but gleaming teeth and a big gator grin,
with absolutely no room left, not even for a gator's chin.
Nonetheless, no matter how it is driven,
one thing is for certain, Santa's sled flying on Christmas Eve will
be a given.
One night, while he slept a dream did appear,
and in it he saw one of Santa's Reindeer.

THE FOR AS YOU SEE TALES

A question was asked and an answer was given,
"Why had Santa sent one of his Reindeer to where he was liven?"
The Reindeer replied, not in a rude or hastily way,
"Santa sent me to check out your pipeline to use as his sled runway."
With that task complete, the Reindeer turned and said bye,
and with a shake of his tail, off he did fly.
Now I know this seems strange, and to some it surely may be,
but to me it is real, just as real as your Christmas tree.
Of course when he awoke, this dream he was quick to reveal,
so now without a single doubt in your mind,
come Christmas Eve around midnight, you will find,
me sitting, waiting for Santa on the pipeline at the bottom of my hill.
Santa came to my Sister and his card she was handed,
and like magic would have it, in Waskom he had landed.
Even stranger it seems upon further inspection,
the phone number on the card required my Sister and I to take a deeper reflection.
With such an everlasting love for Christmas, Mom always kept Santa in our hearts, and now with Mom's old phone number as his, Mom and Santa will never be apart.
Two stories I have told and two true events have taken place,
Now with any luck come Christmas Eve on the pipeline behind my house, I'll get to see Santa's bright rosy red face.
For as you see, when I think of Christmas it is easy to forget,
that the true meaning of Christmas isn't wrapped up in the presents that you get. If you stop shopping long enough to look at the top of the nearest Christmas Tree, You will see the Christmas Angel that lives right next to me.

End of Story

What's Different With Christmas This Year?

A SHORT STORY

At what point does a child grow up? All know scholars of our times have placed that age at the year someone turns 21. I think the age a child really grows up is simply the moment they stop believing.

Way up north were there is snow all year round, lives a pair of green elves. Why green I can only guess, and if I had to make an assumption, it would be because green is Santa's favorite color. If you think about it, green up north is the only color you do not see much of. Any way on to my story.

These two green elves, one named Mine (just leave off the e at the end) and the other named Hours have only one job to do for Santa all year round, but no elves job is more important than the one that keeps track of time that passes from one Christmas to the next. Each second, every minute and all the hours in a day have to be recorded and accounted for. For everyone knows that at the North Pole the Sun doesn't set for months on end. How difficult do you think it would be to know exactly what time it was when it became time to take off in his sled if Santa's clock suddenly stopped ticking? The last time the clock stopped ticking at Santa's house was it the year of the great freeze; I need not remind you of what a messy Christmas that was. Elves running left and right, gifts being left off the sled; nothing but sheer Ciaos and Mayhem (the two smallest elves) left behind to clean up the mess that followed after the Christmas of 1810. Anyway on to my story.

It was the month of May, but you couldn't tell it by looking outside, when in walked another green elf into Elf Central Headquarters. He walked up to the counter where Mine and Hours sat and introduced himself as Sec, then he informed them that he had been given the job right next to theirs. So Mine and Hours welcomed him behind the counter and made a little space for him to sit at the desk by their side. It took about a couple of months before Mine started noticing that something just didn't seem right when he tallied up the minutes and hours of the past day, and so he decide to say something to Hours about it.

Well when Hours looked at the time reading he didn't notice anything different, so Mine just passed his feelings off as being just a little bit of fall fever, something he usually got each year about this time. It only seemed like days; when really months had passed before that feeling of something just wasn't right once again crept up on Mine. This time he pleaded for Hours to take a better look at the timing of the clock, and of course this time the error almost stuck out like a sore thumb. One can only guess as too how long the seconds, one at a time, had been added to each hour that passed by on the clock. Knowing that the only person who could have added the seconds to the clock was the new elf (Sec), the other two calmly walked over and sat down next to him for an inter office meeting. Sec proudly admitted to adding seconds to each day and he joyfully explained that he had done so to adjust for daylight savings time. With all three elves in the same boat, someone had to be chosen to go and tell Santa, and with the short straw being pulled by Hours, he bundled up and prepared for the worst.

KATHY (AE) COX

The trail Hours left in the snow as he trudged over to Santa's house was deep and wide, and as he knocked on the door Santa was heard to say "enter please". Hours opened the door and then knelt at Santa's easy chair when he started telling him of the bad news. Santa only grinned as he put a finger up side his nose. After a minute of silence he said, "you know if you stop and think about it, the only real change that needs to be made is to make my annual stops at Arizona, South America, Africa, and Asia to be last on my list this year instead of first. Since our clock has been changed this year to include Daylight Savings Time. Now go on back home and keep an eye out for the memo I'll be sending you three regarding time changes now and in the future."

The tracks in the snow Hours made back home were as light as a feather, as too was his spirit. The only thing he said as he opened the door was, "Sec, I hope you like noises and confetti, because unless you can prove me wrong, I know where we will be as the ball drops in Times Square this New Years Eve." With a puzzled look on his face Sec looked at Mine and whispered the question, "What does a ball dropping at Times Square have to do with us?" Mine laughed and replied, "Sec my friend that is the only way we can accurately reset our clock."

For as you see, Santa may just be a little bit late delivering your present this year, and I will be more than willing to bet that if you pick up a weekly tabloid sometime after New Years this year, you will read that there has been another Alien sighting of three little green men in New York City as the ball finishes dropping at Times Square this New Year's Eve, and by the way if I forgot to say it, I would like to wish you all a very Merry Christmas and a really Happy (Green) New Year.

End of Story

At The Equator, How Do They Know When It Is Christmas?

A SHORT STORY

Toby never heard his Mom say, "Baby put your coat on, it is cold outside and if you don't you will surely catch your death of a cold". Toby never looked out his window and saw any other color than green on the trees in his back yard. Even without the first signs of winter to clue him into the fact that the seasons were about to change, Toby like all other 5 year olds just knew that Christmas would be coming soon.

A year ago Toby watched as his Mom put up their yearly Christmas palm tree and then helped her decorate it with all the nuts and berries gathered by the both of them just weeks before. Nuts and berries that they had picked up just a few feet from their own back door. Living in a rain forest didn't leave much time for play or much time to decorate a palm tree, so thank goodness there weren't many branches on the palm tree to decorate and thank goodness the nuts and berries didn't weigh much or the branches wouldn't be strong enough to hold them all.

There were no brightly colored bows or fancy string to wrap presents in and the only paper to be found came from the leaves of the giant elephant plants. Most of their leaves were tall enough to hide behind especially when Toby wanted to disappear from sight. Most of the time the toys he received would be something needed to help around the house or help in the fields where his Mom and Dad harvested their crops of Bananas to sell at the local market. One year Toby's present to his surprise was a rake and the next year he received a slightly used wheelbarrow, one that his Dad had been asking his Mom for all the year before.

It seemed that his Dad had needed one forever, but it took a whole year before it was wrapped and put under their tree, so for his Dad to let him play with it at Christmas was in deed a great present to him. One day of being pushed around by your Dad in his very own wheelbarrow was worth waiting for, and then of course, Dad and the wheelbarrow were both off to the fields the very next day.

Toby watched as the palm tree went up and he quickly helped his Mom decorate it since a year had already flown by. Toby being a year older and a year wiser to the next step of having a wrapped present under the tree couldn't wait until his Mom brought the present out and placed it under the tree with his name on it. Being the young man that he was he walked up to it, took a quick survey of its size and approximate weight then went back to his chores. Don't get me wrong, even though he didn't pick it up and shake it with his Mom watching, he snatched it up the first time his Mom's back was turned, because that is what all 5 year olds do.

He thought as he turned the package upside down and then right side up again, "Should I shake it?" "Will it break", "What can it be??" His curiosity got the better of him so he shook it, but heard nothing rattle, as he heard his Mom coming in the back door Toby wisely put the package back in its place safely under the tree.

Christmas Eve had made it and as Toby lay his head down to sleep, the vision of the wrapped present under the tree was the last

THE FOR AS YOU SEE TALES

thing he remembers seeing as his little eyes slowly closed. He barely remembers his Mom and Dad giving him his nightly goodnight kiss, and then hurray, it was Christmas morning. Even if it wasn't Christmas morning, waking up your parents from a deep sleep was almost an impossible task, but a 5 year old on a mission was a force to be reckoned with for sure.

Toby's Mom handed him his usual need only presents and one by one Toby opened them with a smile, then right before she handed him his last one, she told him where it had come from and how special this present would be to all of them. Since it was so special and since it was the last one to open Toby took his time unwrapping it. As the leaves unfolded, the biggest smile came across his face as he looked down at the most brightly colored Frisbee he had ever seen. Not only was it a toy he could play with all year round, it was also a toy that he could share among his closest friends. His Mom smiled as Toby went out to play and then she turned to his Dad and said that next year the wonderful Christian Missionaries had promised her they would return and bring hacky sacks with them this next time. The only problem is I do not know what a hacky sack is? I think it is a toy, what do you think? Toby's Dad replied, "Whatever it is, don't worry we will find a way to play with it."

For as you see, no matter where you are, even a blind man knows when Christmas has arrived. All he has to do is listen for the laughter of the children.

End of Story

Campfire

A SHORT SPOOKY STORY

Halloween has made it and the moon is full. Something spooky is lurking just out of sight at the edge of the dark forest woods.

There is a reason that bats and cats do not carry flashlights. It is safer if you walk in the darkness; than it will ever be for anyone like you; to be sitting out in the open by a lit campfire. Still Toby couldn't bring himself to leave the warmth of the fire, and as he sat there waiting for his Dad to return with more supplies for their weekend camping trip. Toby tried not to pay any attention to all the noises the forest creatures were making. He just kept thinking about the day of fishing his Dad had planned for them the very next morning, and how all of the noises he was hearing didn't really sound all that scary. He would say outloud to himself, "yep that is just you old Mr. Cricket and nice to hear from you Mr. Bullfrog", and then he would take another bite of his sandwich, and wash it down with a drink from his water jug.

Then all of a sudden Toby sat right straight up on the log he was sitting on, he turned his head from side to side to try and locate the

THE FOR AS YOU SEE TALES

noise off in the distance. A noise that he had never heard before, so he slowly placed his sandwich down beside him and picked up his flashlight. He then started scanning the darkness in hopes of seeing what he was really wishing wasn't actually there at all.

He jumped a little bit when the light he was shinning about caught sight of a rabbit eating away on a patch of grass just a few yards away, "but rabbits eat softly" he thought to himself, and the noise he was hearing didn't come from the bunny, "so what could it be"?

Once again he heard the sound, and this time it seemed to be getting louder and closer, it almost made Toby drop his flashlight the second he heard it. "What is that?", Toby mumbled, as he inched closer and closer to the fire burning in the firepit. Then again the noise seemed to shake the silent darkness. Toby sprang to his feet this time. His fear and reflexes made him run off about 100 yards out into the woods. Noises in the woods tend to echo off the rocks and trees.

So when he ran out away from the noise that was haunting him and the campfire, he made certain that he could still see the fire's glow. His fear of being lost in the woods won over his fear of the noise coming increasingly closer to him. With just a few more steps he froze dead in his tracks, just outside the campfire's lights reach.

Toby waited it seemed like hours, but in reality it was only about 5 minutes before his Dad returned from the store. Toby was out of breath as he tried to tell his Dad all that had happened while he was away, but the best part came when they both noticed that their supper sandwiches had all gone missing.

For as you see, not all things that go bump in the night can be explained, and Toby's strange noise now has a craving fetish for peanut butter and jelly sandwiches.

End of Story

Boooooooo, and Happy Halloween to yoooooooou.

93

CHAPTER THREE

FOR THE OLDER CROWD

Doing Time

A SHORT STORY

The whistle blew and of course there was the usual mad dash of workers over to the time clock; all trying to clock out for the end of their morning shift. Thank God the plant had two time clocks, one for the influx of people wanting to clock in and one for those ready to clock out, or the whole place would have to come to a dead standstill with each changing of the shifts. "Shoes For Two" really wasn't that bad of a place to work for and almost every store in our home town carried our line of footwear. It always made me smile when I could say to a total stranger; as I pointed to a pair sitting on the top shelf, "you know what, I made those".

One day as I had stopped for a moment to examine a pair of shoes right before I was ready to add the final stitch to the instep, my boss came over and introduced me to the new guy just hired to work right next to me. I could tell right off the bat from the way he walked in that he was extremely nervous, so to break the ice; even though I was up to my neck in work; I smiled and asked him where he had worked before. Mike was his name and I was taken back when he told me he hadn't worked anywhere else and that this was his first job. I said, "Mike, my name is Kelly and I would like to invite you into my wonderland". "Wonderland", Mike replied, "What do you mean by wonderland?" It was then that I pointed over to Joe who sat just one aisle down to our right. I said, "Well over there is Joe he is the "Mad Hatter" and right next to him is sitting Ned he's the "King of Hearts". They are both very good friends of mine and I have known and worked with them for many years and when we get a break I'll introduce them to you.

Mike looked at me as if I had lost my mind, so of course, I had to try and ease his fears by explaining to him that after hours we were all actors at the local theater and that "Alice In Wonderland" was what we were performing on stage this up and coming weekend.

You could see the stress starting to flow off Mike as he started working next to me, knowing that I hadn't really gone off the deep end of the work pool. As the days went by and we became more and more friends, Mike started feeling more and more at home with his job. It didn't take anytime before he saw that there wasn't a question he asked of me that I didn't know the answer to and not one problem that arose, that I couldn't solve. All I did day after day was talk about wonderland and try to throw myself into the role of "Peter Pan". I guess I forgot to mention that I play the lead role, well anyway on with our story. One day at the end of our shift, Mike looked at me and asked, "Where are we going to be next weekend after you are finished doing "Alice In Wonderland"? That is when I knew our friendship was solid as a rock and I couldn't help but smile when I said "How do you feel about pirate ships and buried treasure?" Mike just smiled and said, "Arrg, matey that's a go, just as long as you are willing to divide up the buried treasure with me 50/50".

For as you see, we all have to work. You can either make each day of work an adventure with friends by your side and the time of 30 years will have flown by in a matter of seconds, or you can make it a dark dreary dungeon in which you are sentenced to life. If you make it a dungeon totally surrounded by fellow inmates with virtually no hope for parole then I am sure you will live to regret it.

What is funny to me though is that the buildings we work in are all the same, just structures made of brick and stone. It is the people inside the buildings that make the difference between <u>working</u> and <u>doing time</u>.

End of Story

A Mother's Tears

A SHORT STORY

Jason's Mother was watching out her front door window when she saw Jason fall off his tricycle. By the time she got to him he was sitting on the concrete with his scraped up knee in his hands and tears coming down his face. His Mom carried him into the bathroom and doctored his scraped knee, put a bandage on it and then kissed it, making it all better as she wiped the tears from his face. Jason quit crying and looked at his Mom with a puzzled look on his face as he asked, "Mommy why are you crying? Your knee is fine and now that you kissed mine it is all better too." His Mom just laughed as she wiped away her tears then she replied, "Baby, I cry when you cry. What hurts you also hurts me, and when you get a booboo on your knee, I get a booboo on my heart."

Years past and Jason came home one day after trying to get a date with Jan. His Mom could tell that she had told him that they were no longer going steady. Jason tried to hide his hurt but no matter how hard he tried to hold it back, his hurting still shone through. His Mom couldn't kiss away this hurt so she just told him to believe her when she said, "And This Too Shall Pass". Then she quietly went to her room, opened her Bible and read it as tears rolled down her face.

Jason grew up and soon had a family of his own. One day when he woke up, something just didn't feel quite right as he sat up in bed, just then the phone rang. As Jason answered the phone the person on the other end told him that his Mom was in the hospital, and that she had fallen and broke her hip. Jason quickly arrived at his Mom's hospital room just as the nurse was giving her a shot of something to ease her pain. Jason hurried to her side and kissed his Mom on her cheek, and gave her a long soft hug. When he backed away his Mom could tell that he was on the verge of tears. That is when she said, "Jason, I will be Ok, so why are you crying?" But before Jason could answer her, she added, "Oh yeah, I know why, Son, it is because Momma's booboo has put a booboo on your heart hasn't it? But you know I'll be all right now that you are here." Jason just smiled, nodded, and then asked her about how long the Doctors expected it to take for her to get better.

For as you see, there is no greater bond than the one between a Mother and her Child, when her baby (no matter how old they are) hurts, a Momma will always be the one who feels the pain and when their Momma hurts, nobody, and I do mean nobody had better stand in her Childs way.

End of Story

A Tale Of Two Sisters

A SHORT STORY

The day the twins were born, their Father could tell they were as different from each other as day and night, and so that is what he named them. The first one to be born was named Day and the second became Night. Then he lifted each one of them up, one at a time to the sky spirit in order to have the sky sprit bless their birth, Day was smiling and cueing at the suns warm embrace, while Night squinted her eyes and then started crying until he held her up under a shade tree.

As they grew older Day was the one who was strong in body, but also very weak in spirit. She would have the endurance and strength of an Ox, but when she saw a little bird with a hurt wing, it would always sadden her to the brink of tears. Night on the other hand couldn't lift a feather, but was tough as nails when it became time to kill the food they needed for the supper table.

Their Father being the Chief of the tribe, had to decide when it was time for his little Princesses to wed. He contacted his neighboring tribe and they sent over a Prince to take his pick of the two maidens. As they stood in front of him in order for him to choose between the two, he gave each a red rose. Day took the rose and held it softly in the palm of her hand, while Night just held it at her side and didn't give it another thought. Of course the prospective groom picked Day to be his bride.

The Day of the wedding arrived, Night was happy for her Sister, but at the same time she couldn't understand why the groom hadn't picked her as his bride and she wondered if she would ever find a husband of her own. Even though she was strong enough in spirit to make it on her own she still needed a strong man to protect her.

The wedding had ended shortly after sundown, so Night started walking and crying while feeling sorry for herself along the path that lead to the cliff's edge. As she stood looking out over the edge at the deep ravine below, she heard a very manly voice tell her that she should be careful as she stood so very close to the edge.

She told the young man, that she would be fine and for him not to worry. He replied that it was his job to worry about such a pretty young girl as herself. He then asked if she wouldn't mind having a seat next to him and tell him what had brought her out to the edge of the cliff at such a late hour.

Night sat down beside her new found friend and asked him his name. He said, "My name is Dusk. What is yours?" Night told him her name and then asked him why he was sitting there. Did he come for the wedding? Dusk replied, "My twin brother "Dawn" is the groom." Night just laughed when she told him that her twin sister "Day" was the bride.

Night and Dusk hit it off right from the bat. Dusk was as strong as an Ox, but when it became time to kill a spider, that dirty job fell on Night's shoulders. Go figure.

For as you see, sometimes a set of Brothers and Sisters will marry a set of Brothers and Sisters. Living happily ever after. Prime examples are: Uncle Paul and Aunt Needy; Aunt Joy and Uncle WD; who are as different and yet exactly the same as Day and Night.

End of Story

An Up Hill Climb

A SHORT STORY

Nothing worth having is easily obtained. The richest of men will always want something they do not have and can never buy with their power, and what they can't buy, will usually always end up being something in the form of happiness.

The King thought he was safe and sound behind his castle walls with all he would ever want or need. The castle sat high on a hill with a whole army of guards standing watch at their post just to stop all who wanted to enter the King's castle. All the King would ever ask for was handed to him on a real silver platter. When he wanted entertainment, the court jester would be summonsed, but even with a smile painted on his face, you could still see that the court jester really didn't want to be there. So after the jester became too tired to perform any longer the King would still be left with the unhappiness that the jester had brought with him.

The day came for the King to pick a Queen, but out of all the choices he had to choose from, none of the maidens standing before him could offer him any degree of happiness. All that shone through was just their fake smiles was their unhappiness as well. So once again the King was denied his happiness.

The bells rang from the castle walls announcing the birth of the next new King to be one day. As the King held his new son in his arms, he suddenly fell to his knees and started to cry out with tears of joy as he unwrapped the cloth from around the babies face to show to all there how beautiful the smile on his Sons face was. It was a smile of true happiness which was something that was priceless in the King's eyes.

For as you see, everything good in life will usually only be found on the top of mountains, and yes, the up hill climb will always be worth the effort. So if you can; always try to do what makes you happy; because true happiness can sometimes be hard to find.

End of Story

Beanie This One Is For You

A Tale Of A Tale

Knock-Knock, Who's there? Tella me. Tella me who? Tella me if you like this one.

It was a nice fall morning as I was walking through the park, minding my own business, I might add, when a man came up to me and asked me what time it was. I stopped walking and so as to not seem impolite I replied, "Sir I'm sorry but I left my watch at the house this morning, but I am pretty sure it hasn't been but about 10 minutes since I left home and I started my walk at exactly 7AM this morning. The man thanked me and then went on his way.

I went only about a few more steps forward when another man came up to me and asked me if I knew what time it was. So once again I explained how I had left my watch at the house and that I had left my house at exactly 7AM this morning and the time I left had to be about 15 minutes ago. The man thanked me and then we both went on our way.

This time I managed to get only about 10 more minutes into my walk when a third man approached me and asked, I knew you would guess it, he asked the pressing question "do you know what time it is?" Well this time instead of being polite, I found myself getting more and more impatient and snappy when I gave him my length reply as to what I estimated the time of day to be. This time when he thanked me, I said nothing back in return.

I was still grumbling under my breath when I rounded the corner of my street and reached the sidewalk in front of my house. That was when my next-door neighbor came out of his house and said, "You seem to be a little bit late getting back from your walk this morning, friend, don't you know what time it is?" That did it, it was all I could take, I let my neighbor have it with both barrels (so to speak) and he hasn't said another word to me since.

The question each man asked of me was the same, and each of them were equally as polite with their asking, so where did my problem with the three men come from? Was the problem all mine or did the problem simply stem from the repetitive nature of the question and in turn the repetitive reply I was being forced to be give to them in return?

For as you see, there is no way I would ever be a Doctor or a Nurse, simply because all the patients that they see days on end ask them the very same questions over and over again, which of course, makes them have to give each one of their patients the same reciprocating reply. I guess the real problem with that scenario is deeply rooted in the fact that each patient they see on a daily bases doesn't seem to realize that they are posing the same questions to the Doctors and Nurses as the patients that went in before them. They see themselves as being the one and only person in the waiting room with that (deer in the headlight) look on their face, but believe me when I tell you they are not.

End of Story

For my Sister
(who has the patience of Jobe)

Bringing Down This Old House

A SHORT STORY

Far out in the middle of nowhere stands what remains of a very stately and once costly plantation manor. The last of its inhabitance had passed away years back without leaving any children as heirs to their estate. The old pre Civil War dated home was in dire need of repairs, all of which would take a whole lot of time and money to accomplish and still not get it back to its original beauty. Although it didn't have all the comforts of modern day living, if someone would just take an interest in seeing to the remodeling it surely wouldn't be beyond repair.

Ralph and Theodore usually would spend every afternoon just before sundown sitting and rocking on the old house's back porch swing. Of course Ralph would call it a porch while Theodore would argue with him and refer to it as their veranda, either way they could usually be found sitting there looking out across the pond just about every evening. Ralph would show up in his usual navy blue and Theodore in his slate gray. Once the sun went down; both of them would sit and decide the order of the day.

Ralph spoke up first and told Theodore that there had been a new sign placed in their front yard. Theodore asked Ralph if he was sure it was a new sign and Ralph replied, "Come around front and see for yourself". Ralph then pointed at the sign as they rounded the corner of the house and there the sign was with this big SOLD strip stretched out across the front of it. When they returned to the swing a whole new topic started to arise. Ralph said, "I thought I heard them say they were going to take up the offer, but I wasn't really sure until now that they had. Theo, I'm afraid this time the house just might be torn down instead of being fixed back up." Theodore argued by saying, "no way, they can't tear down this wonderful manor." Ralph pointed to the side of the house and said, "Do you see where those boards are missing? One just fell off the house yesterday and I couldn't find a hammer or nails. I wish I had come across some, because I would have nailed that board back on myself."

Theodore stopped him from saying any more about the board when he started laughing at Ralph. Ralph said, "What is so funny about that?" Theo replied, "How were you going to lift that board, when we both know I killed you about 140 years ago?" Ralph replied, "You might have shot me, but I shot and killed you first". Theodore disagreed and then added that even if he did shoot him first that the South had won the War Between the States. Ralph cleared his throat and said, "I beg your pardon, but the Civil War was won by the North." Theodore stopped arguing just long enough to ask Ralph what he thought the new owners would do with their house. Ralph hesitated for a moment then spoke up and said, "I overheard someone say something about putting up a shopping mall. Do you happen to know what one of those shopping malls are?" Theodore replied with a "nope, I sure don't. I just hope they don't mind us hanging around."

THE FOR AS YOU SEE TALES

For as you see, who really knows where ghost go once the house that they have lived in for years has to be torn down. They might just move next door and come live with you, or maybe they just might go shopping in your local shopping mall after all the stores in the mall are closed for the night.

End of Story

Excuse Me Please

A SHORT STORY

Some stories come from fact, some from fiction. Most of mine come from perceptions, all of them happen to be my own.

The King's schedule always was a full one, and since it was the first Monday of the month, the King not only had to meet with all the Land Lords in and around his Kingdom; he also had to balance his own royal checkbooks. That was a job he entrusted to no one except himself. As the King entered his throne room he stopped at the door just for a moment in order to reemphasize to his guards standing there just exactly how important it was for him not to be disturbed. He wanted to make sure he wouldn't be bothered, not even for a slit second, for at least the next couple of hours anyway. As he stepped through and shut the door behind him, both guards acknowledged that they totally understood the command he had just given them.

Only thirty minutes had passed before a man about the age of 18 came running down the hall towards the throne room door. Of course as he approached, the guards shouted, "Halt" almost in

THE FOR AS YOU SEE TALES

unison. The young man, in between gasps for air, sharply requested an audience with the King. As per previous instruction the guards denied the young man's entrance. The young man was almost in tears, as he told the guards that what he needed to talk to the King about was of the utmost importance and it couldn't wait. Once again the guards said, "NO".

With not even one ounce of hope left in the young man's heart that he would be able to talk to the King, and knowing how much precious time had already been wasted on his trying, the young man turned around and ran back down the hall. He ran away from the throne room, and then out of the guard's sight. It wasn't but about 5 minutes more before the King opened the door and in a very angry state of mind barked orders to the guards to come and see what was happening just outside the throne room window. As the guards advanced to the open window they couldn't help but notice the two or three really big stones that lay on the floor just in front of the King and lying on the window's ledge.

As one of the guards started to stick his head out the window to look down at the courtyard, he had to dodge another rock as it went sailing past him into the room. The guard was yelling down at the assailer when he realized it was the young man that he had just earlier sent away. The guard told him to stop throwing rocks at the window, and the young man replied, "Not until I see the King." The King was so disturbed and angry for being interrupted that he came to the window himself, just to fuss at the one who would dare to waste his precious time.

As the King leaned out the window and looked down at the young man, the King started to open his mouth and fuss at the young man. That was when the King became startled to find out that the young man who had gone to such great lengths in order to get to see him, was now starting to turn and run away. But before leaving, the young man stopped just long enough to point to the hill at the East edge of the castle walls and then with a loud voice he yelled out to the King, "Don't look now, but we have company", and then he started running away. It wasn't long before the young man had run clean out of sight headed straight towards the <u>West</u> end of the Court Yard. The King took his binoculars and looked in the direction the young man had pointed, and at first he didn't see anything, but before he could put the binoculars down his enemy's army started cresting the East hill. What a difference time and advanced notice can make.

For as you see, The Declaration Of Independence states, "That All Men Are Created Equal". For all you would be Kings out there, that simply means that my time, no matter what you may think of it, is just as equally important to me, as yours is to you.

End of Story

Don Pablo

A Short Story

Now that I think about it, this short story is more of a tale than a story. This tale happened a long time ago, when criminals were very seldom caught, you could take for example, Butch Cassidy and the Sundance Kid. So you see, so goes the tales of Don Pablo.

Don was raised by the best of Mothers, but when his Dad decided to leave them and seek his fame and fortune across the Mexican border, Don's childhood was cut short. This left his Momma alone to raise him all by herself. Without a father figure around Don started running with the local gangs. Don learned fairly young that a life of crime would always pay you more than any pay he could manage to make from working on his family's farm. As with all monies not earned honestly, the price you finally have to pay just to keep it is always too high a price to pay.

Don soon became the leader of the gang. His strength and willingness to protect his turf from all other gangs was taking its toll on him. Don's second in command and his only trusted friend, Juan, always met with Don at the local cantina every Friday night. Just after dark they would talk things over about how much business was at hand for the weekend, and who needed to have the fear of "Don" put into them.

Juan immediately noticed that something wasn't quite right with Don as he limped into the bar that night. Don looked overly tired and worn out, and on the verge of shear exhaustion. Juan knew he couldn't ask too many questions of his friend, but still he needed to let him know he was a little bit concerned about his health. Don had lost an eye fighting off a rival gang in the years following his 30th birthday. He had lost several toes on his right foot from running from the federal government as they chased him back over the border a few years back. Don had a price on his head, so if he ever decided to cross the border again; he might not make it back home so he didn't wander far from home anymore.

As Don sat down and started to take a drink of his beer, Juan asked him how he had been feeling lately. Don said, "Juan, I can't do this any longer." Juan then couldn't help but ask, "My friend, what is wrong?" Don started shaking as he started telling Juan that he was going to turn himself into the border police. Juan lowered his voice and then said, "But Don, why would you want to do such a thing?" Don replied, "The nightmares are too much for me to handle. I can't sleep much and when I do, it is nothing but one bad dream after another." Don went on to say, "Juan do you remember me telling you about what my Momma had told me the last time I saw her? She told me that if I didn't change my ways, then when she died she would come back and haunt me?" Juan said, "Vaguely, why?" Don said, "Well the nightmares started up a few months ago. The first time it happened I just blew it off, but when the nightmares started coming more often I finally got the message loud and clear. So tomorrow, I am going to turn myself into the authorities."

Juan asked, "What are the nightmares about?" Don said, "They are basically all the same, they start with me being a little boy in my Momma's lap while she rocked me back and forth in her rocking chair. She is telling me over and over again that she knows she taught me better than that, and I needed to be a better good boy.

THE FOR AS YOU SEE TALES

When I wake up, I am sitting in my bed just rocking myself back and forth, back and forth, as I say out loud, OK Momma."

Juan looked puzzled as he told Don that maybe he should turn himself in. Juan said, "I think I need to turn myself in right along with you, because I am starting to have nightmares of my own". Then Juan said, "My nightmares are just a little bit different though". He told Don that he dreamed that he was a snake crawling around on his stomach just minding my own business. As he crawled out from under a rock suddenly this big eagle swoops down and picked him up in its claws. Then the snake just flew off carrying him away to its nest. That was when they both looked up at the Mexican flag hanging over the bar and Juan said, "Whoa, our flag sure has a big eagle with a snake held tightly in its claws on the front of it. It looks like the snake that carried me away in my nightmares. Maybe it's time for the two of us to go to the police station and come clean of our crimes. Then with any luck our nightmares will stop".

For as you see, How many people do you think are behind bars today just simply because they had a guilty conscious and couldn't fight the resulting lack of sleep that comes from the guilt they held for so long? **A whole lot more than you would think** I'm sure.

End of Story

How Special Are You?

A SHORT STORY

It was about lunchtime when the man entered the watch repair shop. The old repair shop owner walked over to the counter and asked the man how he could help him. The man explained that he had just inherited this very old antique gold watch from his Grandfather. His Grandfather had told him that he had gotten it from his Grandfather, so the man wasn't quite sure exactly how old it truly was. The man told the store owner that he wanted him to get the watch ready to be stored in a house safe so when his little boy became old enough it could be pasted down to him one day. The owner said, "I have never seen a watch than beautiful before." He then said that he should be paying him instead, for the honor of being able to work on such a treasure. The owner said, "Does twenty dollars sound fair?" The man replied, "That is more than fair, when should I return for the watch?" The owner said, "Just give me one full day."

The man left the watch and a phone number where he could be reached if needed. The owner started to work on opening the watch right away. He had all of the pieces lying out on his workbench when

THE FOR AS YOU SEE TALES

he heard the door open up and another customer come in. As he turned around to get up from his worktable, his knee struck the leg of the table so hard that it made the table shake. All the pieces of the watch moved, but only one piece rolled away and ended up just under the edge of a book the owner had laid near the edge of the table.

When it came to a stop rolling around, the littlest gear piece asked the rest of the watch pieces "hey guys, what just happened? Was it an earthquake?" The rest of the group replied "I'm not sure, but I hope it doesn't happen again, because we almost lost you over the edge." It wasn't long before the owner returned to finish his job of cleaning the watch. With each gear piece that he placed back into the case, it became increasing obvious that he was going to overlook the littlest piece. When the owner was once again distracted the littlest piece yelled out "guys, I think he doesn't know I have rolled over here under his book and I think he will finish his work without me going back into the watch."

He then started to panic and said "guys can any of you think of anything we can do to let him know that he is about to leave me behind?" The group was saddened to have to tell him that he indeed might be overlooked. At the same time they pointed out that even though he was the littlest piece, he was one of the most important pieces. He alone was the piece that made the watch chime every hour on the hour and without him the watch would be silent forever.

The owner finished closing the watch and wrapped it up for delivery the next day. The man came and went with his watch working and keeping time as it had always done. It didn't take but little over an hour later for the man to return, and tell the owner that something was missing from the watch and would he please recheck it. After a closer look the owner noticed the missing little piece and when he found it under the book he placed it back where it belonged. The watch chimed over and over again as if it were trying to make up for lost time.

117

For as you see, even the smallest things on this planet are needed to make the world whole. A world without ants to clean up some of the waste we just throw out our car windows would be a planet with more of a smell to it.

I hate fire ants, but I love fire ants in the same breath.

End of Story

That Was A Really Good Bad Dream

A SHORT STORY

As you would have guessed the North Pole is quite busy this time of year. All the Elves were working long hours trying to please their bosses while also trying to make sure each department production quota came out looking its very best. Randy was no exception, he put his whole heart and soul into his work, so when he finally did get to go home to his wife Tina all she would have time to do was feed him. Then they would both have to go straight to bed just so he could wake up early enough to go right back to work the next day.

Randy was asleep just about the minute his head hit his pillow. Tina climbed into the bed right behind him. He had already started snoring so she just lay there and thought about what she needed to do to get ready for the up and coming Christmas Day Feast at Santa's house. Tina usually brought warm homemade banana pudding, but since the bananas were kind of scarce this year she thought she might have to change and make mince meat pies instead. Just when she was going to softly shake Randy awake and ask him if there would be enough raisins for her pies, she stopped for a moment and then she suddenly poked him in the ribs instead, which immediately jarred him awake.

Startled Randy sat up and asked Tina just what was the reason for her poking him in the ribs, and waking him up. With a big smile on her face Tina replied, "I had to wake you up quickly because you were having such a very **bad** dream." Randy said, "Bad dream, bad dream, I don't remember having a bad dream. I remember my dream being a really good one with Santa calling me into his office and offering me the new CEO's job (Chief Elf Organizer). It included an increase in pay plus a lot less hours to work and then, oh yeah, I remember Santa saying he was going to send me on an all expense paid vacation to Hawaii. Just so I could sit in the sun on the beach and watch the girls as SI magazine was doing a new photo shoot for their next years swim suit issue cover page."

Tina said, "Randy, OK see I told you, you were having a really good <u>bad</u> dream. I could tell your dream was a bad one by the very big grin you had on your face. Now go back to sleep I'll wake you in the morning, that is, if I don't strangle you before then."

For as you see, my husband doesn't get away with being even the least little bit bad; not even in his own dreams.

End of Story

No Pain Means No Gain

A SHORT STORY

One day John opened up his front door, and at the same time he suddenly realized that with each day that went by; he was finding it getting increasingly harder and harder for him to walk to the end of his driveway and then bend over and pick up his morning paper. The driveway hadn't gotten any longer and of course the newspaper didn't shrink so the only thing that had to have changed was John's increasing age with decreasing agility. Every step was a chore and each reach for the newspaper produced a low but still undeniable groan just from the effort it took on John's part to retrieve his morning newspaper. Then upon straightening himself back upright, there was that equally endless walk back into the house for him to look forward to. Thank God it would take hours of sitting in his recliner, drinking his coffee, reading the morning paper, before once again he would be forced to rise up and walk over into the kitchen. Then he would reach up into the kitchen cabinet for his midday snack and soft drink. The energy to do all of those things had to come from somewhere, so logic told him he needed desert. Yes desert, in the form of a honey bun to top off his lunch.

All the effort of the morning has managed to make him tired and the high number of carbs he consumed has made him sleepy, so he falls asleep in his recliner for just a couple of hours or so. He then awakens in just enough time to watch all his evening soaps and talk shows. After the evening news has finished, it becomes time for him to fix his usual supper of sugarcoated cereal floating in a big bowl of whole milk. His primetime evening seven o'clock shows are on now and are soon to be followed by his eight, then nine o'clock shows ending of course with the ten o'clock news. How time flies when you are doing absolutely nothing, and unfortunately time is all our lives are made of. John somehow manages to get up out of his chair just in time for him to go off to his bed for the night. Then wake up and start his next day off in exactly the same way he had started this one.

The next morning though this time when John reached down for his newspaper something unexpected happened. This time, John found himself unable to straighten himself back up. John's neighbor called 911 and John was rushed to the ER. The Orthopedic Doctor on call told John, that if he didn't change his lifestyle and get in better shape that within a matter of months that he would have to go into a nursing home and be in a wheelchair at the ripe old age of 55. John said, "Doc what ever it takes, I will do it, sign me up." The Orthopedic Doctor smiled and said it won't be easy and there will be some pain involved, but if you do nothing there will still be pain only in a different form.

Day one of Physical Therapy came and by the end of the hour, John couldn't even wiggle his little finger without it hurting him. The treadmill was torture, the weight lifting was torture and the stretches would make even a grown man cry. John did cry, but just on the inside so no one could see how much pain he was in.

Day two of Physical Therapy came and by the end of the hour, John pleaded for the therapist to make the pain and torture come to an end, but of course the therapist had different ideas and just added more weights and more time to John's workout.

By day three John was ready to give up and call off any future therapy, and so all the way down the driveway to get his newspaper you could hear John commenting out loud about how hard a work out the therapy was. Then he complained about how sore his muscles were, and if it got any harder he just wasn't going back to the gym. It was then that John noticed when he looked down, that he had his paper in his hand and he was back at his front door in less than the time it took to utter all his words of malcontent. "Wow" is all John said next.

It wasn't long before you would find John walking around the block each morning before he took his paper inside and it wasn't long before John found himself paying extra money just so he could workout for more than just an hour each day.

For as you see, why does most medicines that is good for you have to taste so bad and why can't there be any gain without first having to pay the price of pain? No pain truly means no gain. You know, John and I have a lot in common, we share the same therapist, and by the way, did I happen to mention to you the fact that my right knee hurts?

End of Story

Now, Was That So Hard?

A SHORT STORY

How hard can it be to raise a teenager, is the question Jan asked her Mother as she sent her 12 year old Son out the front door. He had his lunch box in hand and was running off to catch the school bus. It had just stopped in front of her house to pick him up for school. Her Mother laughed as she reminded Jan that "what goes around comes around". Even though she didn't remember what it was like when she was a teenager; her Mother was quick to point out that she hadn't forgotten exactly what Jan's teenage years were like from a Mother's point of view. With that said, her Mom ended the phone conversation by wishing Jan a whole lot of luck with the next seven teenager years that she had ahead of her.

Five years past, and with each year that went by, Jan's Son (Jimmy's) room became more and more messier, with more and more clutter being added to the already over crowded 17 year olds room. As with all good Mothers, all Jan asked of Jimmy was that he clean up his room at least once a week. At first Jimmy would do his best to pick up after himself, but it didn't take very long before he realized that his Mom would come in behind him, and finish cleaning up whatever mess he conveniently left behind. Jan tried to have patience with her Son, and even went so far as to place all the things she wanted put away on top of his bed for him to see. That didn't work because when she would go back into his room the very next day all that she had piled up so nice and neatly on his bed was now pushed off onto the floor beside it. The next step was to throw all the clutter into Jimmy's closet, making it impossible for him to get to his clothes until he did something with the mess. Once again that failed to get his attention, since all he had to do was wear the same old pair of jeans and shirt over and over again; which just happened to be what teenagers his age were doing as a craze. I guess just so they didn't have to clean up their rooms either.

All attempts on Jan's part seemed to be failing, up until she remembered what her Mom had said to her those 5 years back, the words, "I haven't forgotten your teenage years, and what goes around comes around" kept popping up in her head.

With desperation in her voice, she called her Mom in for some advice on the matter. At the kitchen table the two Moms converged with only one thought in mind, (how to teach a teenager boy he needs to keep his room clean). A hard goal to reach, but not impossible Jan's Mom assured her, by saying, "this is what you have to do". Like with a Venus flytrap, the plan was made and the trap was set.

After leaving the school bus and walking his girlfriend (Angie) back across the street to her house, Jimmy stopped at the front door of his house. On the door was a big sign that said, "GARAGE SALE TOMMORROW". Jimmy thought it to be more than just a little bit strange that there was a sign for a garage sale on his front door. Most of the time his Mom would be going to the sales instead of have one, as a matter of fact to the best of his knowledge, this would be the first time that his Mom would want to have one of her own. Jimmy thought out loud, garage sale, that wouldn't bother me; I'll just find something else a whole lot better for me to do. Still it did seem like a really odd thing for his Mom to be doing. He kept that strange feeling all the way up the stairs, and up until he opened up his bedroom door. "Shock and awe" would be a mild description of how Jimmy felt when he opened his door and found nothing in his room except a twin bed mattress lying centered slap dab in the middle of his now empty room.

The words, "**MOM, what have you done?**" could be heard ringing all the way out of the house and into the back yard where of course Jan was standing steadily setting up display tables. The tables were being set up to prepare for her garage sale that was scheduled for early am the very next morning shortly after daybreak. Jimmy flew down the stairs and when he reached the back yard his Mom calmly explained to him that she was going to sell all of the things that he no longer seemed to care anything about. Especially all the things that he never kept clean or wanted it seemed bad enough for him to make an effort to bend over and pick them up off his dirty bedroom floor. It was then that Jimmy noticed his $1000 drum set sitting in the garage with a "$10 or best offer" sign sitting on it. The next words of course that he said were, "Mom, I'm sorry".

For as you see, unless you use a stick of dynamite, most mountains will not come down. Some things can't be put off until tomorrow, and I know your Mom's patience with you will only last just so long before she snaps you back into the real world.

End of Story

Pandora's Box

A SHORT STORY

Legend has it that anyone who found the map should take it and burn it. Burning it would make sure that no one could ever search for its hidden treasure. For if they chose to follow the map then whoever did; would never make it back out of the cave alive. No one can know the secrets that the cave holds deep within it, but who is afraid of a little legend anyway?

Ted and Dave came to the long lost Araneae Mines of Central America just as the map had instructed. Even though Ted would be the one to film the events that pasted; Dave wanted to claim the glory of being the first man to step foot in the hidden room. They were still partners and as equal partners they would share what they found 50/50. Ted stood as still and quite as he could with the camera steadily recording as Dave finally broke through the wall of the cave. Dave narrated each step that he took as he removed the last stone blocking his view of the chamber and the treasure that he expected to find. It was a treasure that has been hidden from man since before the beginning of time. Dave shinned his light into the opening as the last stone fell to the floor in front of him and all he could say was, "Ted it must be full of diamonds and gold, because all four walls seem to light up with radiance that I have never seen before. Help me remove more of the rock so I can squeeze into the opening I need to get a closer look at these walls."

Ted put his camera down and with just a flashlight to go by, both of the men worked and worked until Dave had enough of an opening with which to wiggle his way inside. Ted stood at the opening and kept filming as Dave slowly walked across the wide cavern floor. The walls were just as Dave had described them. As soon as the walls came within his reach, he held out the palm of his left hand to touch its simmering surface. Dave said, "Ted come here and feel", but before he finished his sentence he stopped talking and looked at Ted. Then he yelled, "No, Ted don't come in here". Ted froze in his tracks and then shouted, "Dave what is wrong?" Dave had a panicked look on his face as he slowly said, "I can't remove my hand from the wall.

My palm is stuck against the wall and the more I struggle to free myself the more it glues me to it." Dave then said, "Please go and find us some help, but promise me you won't be gone very long." Ted dropped his camera and quickly told Dave just to stay there and he would hurry back as soon as he could. Dave replied, "Oh yeah, sure thing, of course I'll be here waiting, because at this moment, if I could leave I would. I definitely would rather be out there with you right now, than in here stuck to this wall."

Help was only minutes away even though it seemed like hours for Ted. With a group of about 10 men Ted reentered the mine and headed to the spot where he thought he had left Dave. The men stopped when they all came to Ted's camera lying on the cave floor. All of the men started asking Ted just where the opening to the room was. With his camera in his hand Ted said, "The opening was right here." All the men searched and searched with their flashlights combing every inch of both walls for about 100 feet in each direction. Then one of them decided to question Ted as to if they had used a map to find the location to the hidden room. Ted gasped for a

THE FOR AS YOU SEE TALES

minute then replied, "Yes, we had a map but Dave always insisted on keeping it in his own pocket just for safe keeping."

For as you see, man has always thought that all prehistoric creatures were long gone by now. That is, of course, up until they caught a prehistoric Coelacanth in a fishing net just off the southern coast of Africa. Surprise, Surprise, so why couldn't there be prehistoric spiders still lurking in dark places in South America, and if so I can only imagine how sticky and strong It's web would have to be just to catch and hold a small dinosaur and / or man. So if a prehistoric cockroach and a fish could make it to our present day, then why not a spider, you see these are the things Legends are made of.

End of Story

Raining On Your Parade

A SHORT STORY

They say misery loves company, and whoever first made that astute observation hit the nail right on the head. Some people thrive on having a bad day and they will go out of their way just to make sure your day ends up in exactly the same way. Take this short story for example.

Let us say her name is "Lisa" just to keep her real name completely anonymous. The bank where she works has two bosses that are as different as day and night. One boss is always positive and comes into work with a smile on her face, full of energy, and that boss makes the day go by so fast. So fast that you have to stop your head from spinning around and around just so you can drive yourself home at the end of your day. The other one, on the other hand is totally negative, never smiles, and makes the day drag by so slowly that you can actually watch your hair getting grayer as the day drags on. That boss never has anything up lifting to talk about, and the topics of her conversations are always about the worse things that could possibly have happened. The two bosses

THE FOR AS YOU SEE TALES

come into work on alternating days so they are never there on the same day which makes one day just as bright and sunshiny as a spring day, while the very next day will be a totally rained on and all gloom and doom one.

I started noticing, No, No, No, I mean <u>Lisa</u> started noticing, that every other day she would wake up wanting to stay in bed and call in sick. Also the dread could be seen on Lisa's face when she came into work on the dreadful days. The stress of anticipating the up and coming bad day would force Lisa to clinch her teeth so tightly that it would tend to give her a headache and make her just that much more miserable.

So, you ask, what could Lisa possible do to keep her sanity and stay working at her place of employment? The answer came in the form of short stories, ones that took her mind to happier places, the places that my short stories take me to now. The miserable boss even wanted to control Lisa's thoughts and daydreams, but that is where Lisa drew the line.

When her miserable boss told her to stop thinking about her next story, Lisa told her that her stories and her happy place (which is one and the same), was totally out of her bosses' control and that she couldn't make her stop thinking about whatever Lisa wanted to think about. Nothing else was said about the matter and try as she may, Misery, can't enter into play, and spoil the game, when Lisa is in her **story zone super bowl**.

For as you see, what people get out of making someone else miserable is beyond me. Lisa will always love to work with one boss, and hate working with the other, sad but true.

End of Story

131

Smelling The Roses

A SHORT STORY

High on top of a mountain lives a wise old man. All the people in the valley below know him and at one time or another each of them have taken the long journey up to the top of his mountain. Once someone has gone to all the trouble to reach him, the wise old man would always take the time needed to stop and share his wisdom with them, making sure that before they left each of them would have a total understanding of the advice that he had just given them.

One day at dawn a young man came to the wise old man with a searing question on his mind. He asked, "How can I become rich?" The old wise man was sitting in his chair overlooking the valley below when he replied," Son, that will be a hard one for me to answer, since I, myself have never been a poor man, but for your sake I will give it all my thoughts and efforts. For you to become rich, you will have to put all your heart, and soul into making money." The young man looked puzzled that the answer was so easy, but even so he still thanked the old wise man before he left. As the young man turned to go the old one said, "just remember one thing, when you get the riches you seek, it will still take all your heart and soul just to keep those riches. If you take your eyes off the money for any length of time it will flow away from you like grains of sand in your hand, and before you know it you will be poor once again."

About noon another young man came to the mountaintop with the question, "How can I become famous?" The old wise man was lying down on a blanket looking up at the clouds this time, and so he had to sit up as he replied, "Son, that will be a hard one for me to answer, since my name has always been known for miles around, but for your sake I will give it a try. For you to become famous you will have to put all your heart and soul into getting your fame." This young man also looked puzzled that the answer was so easy, but still he thanked the old wise man before he left. As this young man turned to leave, the old one said, "just remember one thing, when you do get famous it will still take all of your heart and soul just to keep your new found fame. If you stop even for one moment, then soon everyone will stop looking at you, and just like the flickering light of a candle, before you know it, your bright glow of fame will be gone."

Just at sundown another much older man came to the mountaintop with wrinkles on his brow. He looked exhausted so before he could ask his question the wise old man said, "I know you have come to ask me what it takes to become rich and famous." The middle aged man quietly said, "No Sir, I'm sorry but my question contains neither the need for wealth nor fame, because you see I am both extremely rich and extremely famous. What I seek is more complicated than that. In fact I was barely able to escape from my fans and bodyguards even for the little time it has taken me to reach your mountaintop."

The wise old man said, "I'm sorry, Son, I do not leave my home very often. I live a very simple life, one without a Radio or TV." The middle aged man said, "Please sir, "How do I find inner peace?" The wise old man just smiled, and said nothing; instead he just pulled up another chair, and put it along side his. Then he offered the second chair to the middle aged man. As the middle aged man sat down he couldn't help but comment on how beautiful the slowly setting sun looked as it disappeared behind the mountains off in the distance, and then both of them quietly just sat there smiling.

For as you see, the path to inner peace can only come when you allow yourself the time it takes to stop, and smell the roses when you feel the need to. For what kind of life would you have if your every waking moment had to be shared with bodyguards, stalkers, and of course the ever-present paparazzi with their telescoping lens? I am glad the life I chose for myself gives me the time I need to stop and smell the roses.

End of Story

For my Brother Bill & Dorothy

Genie In A Bottle

A SHORT STORY

Mat was strolling down the beach when he came across a bottle floating just off shore. He waded out to get it hoping it contained a letter that maybe someone had written then set a drift for him to find. Instead when he opened it out popped a Genie. Mat was so surprised that he dropped the bottle and broke it on the sand. The Genie was a little bit shaken up about the loss of his bottle, but he still held true to his mission by asking Mat what his first wish would be. Mat thought for a moment then said, "You mean to tell me you are a real Genie, and you are going to grant me three wishes." The Genie replied, "Why yes Master, I am at your command. Just remember three wishes are all I can grant you."

Mat was sitting down on the beach with the Genie in front of him when he made his first wish. He said, "I wish I could relive my life over again." The Genie said, "Your wish is my command." After the smoke cleared Mat found himself back out in the water with the Genie's bottle in his hand. After he opened it back up the Genie told him to try and not drop the bottle this time, and that he still had two wishes left, but before making his second wish Mat asked the Genie what had gone wrong with his first. The Genie told him that he hadn't specified how much of his life he had wanted to relive. So as Mat sat on the beach again he made his second wish, "I wish I could relive <u>all</u> my life over again." The Genie said, "Your wish is my command." This time Mat found himself still sitting on the beach looking right at the Genie when he asked the Genie what had gone wrong with the second wish. The Genie quickly replied, "You didn't specify how fast you wanted to relive your life, and so to save time I let you relive it <u>all</u> in the blinking of an eye."

This time Mat really put some thought into how he would ask for his third wish. When he was ready he told the Genie, "I wish I could relive <u>all</u> my life over again at the <u>same</u> number of days and nights that I have lived it in my past." The Genie said, "Your wish is my command, but if you don't mind my asking I would just like to know why you have wished for the same thing for all three wishes that I granted you." Mat replied, "I want to relive my life, and make all the bad choices I have made in my past into good choices", after saying that Mat vanished. The Genie just shook his head from side to side and said out loud, "I really didn't have the heart to tell him that when he made his last wish, he forgot to include the need to make any changes".

For as you see, live your life without the need for any changes, so that when the bottle of opportunity floats past you, your last wish will not be filled with regret for having wasted all your other wishes on regrets.

End of Story

For Kelly

Swimming With The Fishes

A SHORT STORY

Gary was looking for a job in the classified section of his morning paper when he read about an opening at the local zoo for an experienced scuba diver. The job offered great pay, but the only draw back was it would be just part time, even with only a few hours offered to him he would still be able to make more money than if he was to take a full time job at the local fast food restaurant, so he decided to go to the zoo and apply for the job.

It wasn't until his first day on the job that he found out exactly what he had been hired to do. The shark tank was a pretty big one, and Gary's job turned out to be just keeping the glass tank walls clean so all the people that visited the zoo could see the shark. The one and only shark the zoo could afford to keep in its aquarium was just a baby and when the zoo got it the shark was only about 1 foot long. Gary cleaned the tank every Friday at 6PM like clockwork right after the zoo had closed for the night. At first the baby shark was so cute and shy that Gary decided to make friends with it by bringing a small fish to feed it each time he came to do his job of cleaning its tank. At first the shark kept his distance, but after a couple of cleanings the shark soon gave in and started eating the fish that Gary brought each week. At first it would only get the fish from a distance from Gary, but soon the shark got to where it would take the fish right out of Gary's hand, and Gary watched as the shark grew longer and bigger; so of course the fish Gary brought got bigger along with the shark.

One Friday Gary went into the tank to do his job and as usual he had the shark a nice size fish to eat, but this time something seemed different when he took the fish out of its container to give to the shark, the shark hesitated for a minute before it came over to greet Gary. Something told Gary not to hold the fish out in his hand this time, but to just let the fish float to the surface instead. As the fish floated to the surface Gary could see the shark coming out towards it out of the corner of his eye. The shark went to the surface and came within inches of the fish, but didn't eat it. Instead the shark turned and headed straight for Gary.

Gary could tell by the way it was swimming that the shark wanted to really eat him instead, so he hid behind a near by rock as the shark passed back and forth in front of him. It seemed like hours before the shark finally decided to go to the surface and eat the fish.

Only then did Gary feel safe enough to make his way back out of the tank. The next day Gary gave his resignation and told his boss he could no longer swim in the shark tank. His boss asked him what had happened to make him so afraid of the shark all of a sudden. Gary only said, "I could tell by the look in his eyes that he will one day eat me if he gets another chance. So the only thing I can do is make sure he doesn't get that chance. Sorry but I have to QUIT." All his boss could say was, "I'm sorry you are leaving but I have to tell you that you are a bigger man than I am, because I never would have gone into a tank with a shark no matter what size it was."

THE FOR AS YOU SEE TALES

For as you see, when you swim with the fishes you have to expect that at least one of them will end up being a shark ready to take a bite out of you. So always be aware, be very aware.

End of Story

That's Mine

A SHORT STORY

Since the Stepmother is not the wicked one in this Cinderella story, I feel free to tell you that this story has a definite twist to it.

Jody had remarried a very rich man after her first husband had passed away rather suddenly following a job related accident. The insurance company had paid her a considerable amount for her loss, but still the money didn't fill the hole that was left in her heart after he died, only her remarriage to Stedford could fill that void. Stedford was also quite rich beyond his means, but his wealth, unlike hers, came from his family inheritance that was passed down from generation to generation. Stedford had brought all four of his kids into his home at a very young age to finish raising them in the matter to which he was accustom, and so because of that; he needed a wife like Jody to help him with that job. Jody was the best of Stepmothers, but since the kids were all born with such a big silver spoon in their mouths, they didn't give her anything but trouble when it became time for her to lay their Dad to rest. It aged Jody greatly to have to fight the kids over every little bit of possessions she finally managed

THE FOR AS YOU SEE TALES

"by law" to end up with, and when it was all said and done she was forever saddened from the fight. That has brought us up-to-date on this story, and so it is now time to tell you how this story will end.

Jody wasn't alone when she took her last breath, and so when she felt the time of her death was close at hand, she asked for just the four Adult Stepchildren to be at her bedside. As she strained to utter her last words all she said to them was, "Call my Lawyer, Mr. Jones," and then she passed away.

A few days after the funeral her attorney Mr. Jones received a phone call from Jody's oldest Stepson. Mr. Jones informed him that Jody had requested that he meet with all her Stepchildren and that they were all to be present at the time the meeting was to be held. The meeting was arranged, and like Mr. Jones expected all four of Jody's grown Stepchildren were more than just a little bit fashionably late.

Mr. Jones secretary escorted them into his office and showed them the four chairs that were placed in front of his desk. As each of them took a seat, they couldn't help but notice a chair way off in the back of the room that looked like it had a very old, and stately looking woman sitting there very quietly with her eyes closed as if she were meditating or sleeping; it had to be one of the two.

Before Mr. Jones could even introduce himself, one of the four asked rudely, "Who is she, and why is she here?" Mr. Jones patiently replied, "She is here at your Stepmother's request," and then he left it at that. He continued by telling them that they were all brought to this meeting for a very special purpose, which would be revealed to them all before the meeting was completed. Then before he could say another word, one of the four barked, "Well if you have called us here to talk about anything other than our Stepmother's will then you are wasting all of our time as well as all of your own." Mr. Jones took in a deep breath and then informed them all that Jody had arranged for them to have this meeting far in advance. He then said, "Now if I can continue with this meeting, I would like to inform you as to what I will need from the four of you. Since Jody never remarried and never

141

had any children of her own, you all may want to tell me just exactly what Jody said she had wanted you to have at the time of her death."

As the room got quite, and the four looked at each other, you could see the greed starting to swell in each of their eyes. Then as the arguments started mounting and mounting over which one of them would get the most expensive car, and which one would get all the jewelry, and how they would equally divide the money she had in her numerous bank accounts, no one noticed that, all the while they were discussing the property among themselves. Mr. Jones was steadily writing everything down on his notepad. Not only was he taking an accurate account of what the four Adults said that they wanted; he was also taking an accurate account of what the four of them said what they had already taken out of her house without anyone else knowing what they had secretly gotten away with.

When it seemed as if the four of them had argued enough and had come to a meeting of their minds, Mr. Jones stopped writing, and then quickly introduced the little old woman sitting in the chair in the back of the room as, Madam Linda.

He softly told them that the meeting they were having was really a séance being held by the world renowned spiritual psychic advisor and medium, Miss Madam Linda. She was there just so the spirit of Jody could be present when he informed them as to whom she had chosen to be the executor of her Estate.

Madam Linda who was sitting quietly in the chair in the back of the room started laughing softly as Mr. Jones told all four of them that their Stepmother had chosen a man that lived in another state to have complete control over her earthly possessions. It was then that Mr. Jones, himself, couldn't hold a straight face any longer and so the increasing grin started shining through. It was then that Madam Linda started laughing louder and louder as one of the four of them said out loud, **"Oh crap it's Uncle Bob, she has chosen Uncle Bob to be her executor."** Mr. Jones with a smile still on his face informed the four stepchildren that a written summary of their meeting would be forwarded to the executor of Jody's estate. You should have seen their faces, it was priceless.

THE FOR AS YOU SEE TALES

For as you see, there is just a very fine, thin, and delicate curtain between life and death. One in which neither money nor wealth is able to pass through. Only Joy and Love is allowed to go with you when it becomes your time to draw back the curtain and see what death holds for you on the other side.

End of Story

The Extra Mile

A SHORT STORY

Jake's farm sits nestled at the foot of a beautiful hillside with a clear running stream only a few feet away. Each morning Jake will get up early, before sunrise, just so he can start gathering up all the eggs his hens had laid the night before. Each morning as he gathers their eggs he would sing to them a little song just his own little ditty.

One day Jake added another chicken coop to his farm. It wasn't next door to his older one, yet still it was close enough to hear what the chickens in the newer coop were saying. All was well and life on the farm went on as usual up until one day Sadie noticed that the farmer had stopped singing to them and then started singing the minute he walked into the new chicken coop. Sadie called a meeting with all the other hens and asked them what they thought she could do to try and make the farmer happy again. Josie spoke up and said that she noticed a change in the farmer also. She said, "You all know that I can only lay one egg at a time, and up until that new chicken coop was added, my one egg made the farmer smile at me. Now each time he sees my one egg he looks at me with a frown. To top it off the stress from trying to lay more eggs is making all my feathers fall out". Sadie smiled and told them that she had a plan.

The very next morning when the farmer came to gather eggs he found three eggs in Josie's nest, which immediately put a smile back on the farmer's face and a song back into his heart. Then one day the farmer came to gather eggs a little bit early, and in Josie's nest he found Sadie sitting trying to lay an egg. The farmer quickly shooed Sadie off the nest, because that wasn't where she belonged, and so once again the farmer stopped singing simply because he knew that it wasn't Josie who had tried to please him, it was Sadie instead.

Now, no matter how many times Sadie added eggs from that point on the farmer still wasn't pleased, because he knew no matter where the eggs were laid, the egg count from the coop would always stay the same.

For as you see, it is hard to go the extra mile, if when you stick your foot out to take the first step in that direction, you find out it will land directly on top of the question, "Why?"

End of Story

The Hand Is Quicker Than The Eye

A SHORT STORY

Haven't you ever wondered how a Con Artist is able to Con someone with more than just your average IQ. Well I am here to tell you that the reason the Con Artist is so successful is because that is exactly what they are, they are Artist, and the picture they paint in your mind will make you believe everything they are telling you, which includes the line of Bull they are trying to sell. Case in point is my next story.

New York City is the hub of the world. There is every kind of person standing on every street corner trying to convince you that what they are peddling your way is something you just can't live without. Then there are those who just want you to roll the dice with little too no chance of your winning or even breaking even. So why do people gamble?

Standing behind his small table stood a tall dark haired man. In front of him were four paper cups turned upside down. Three of the cups were placed directly in front of him with the fourth one slightly pushed off to his left hand side. When someone would

THE FOR AS YOU SEE TALES

become curious enough to stop and hear what he has to offer, the conversation will go something like this. "If you can guess which cup the ball is under then you will win, it's just that easy." The Gambler will then either make a wager or he will walk away. If the Gambler stays then the moment the bet is made the Con Artist will have already won.

Money is placed on the table and then the dark haired man will start to move the three cups around and when the cups come to a stop the Gambler will lift one of the cups and low and behold there will be a ball under it, and to no ones surprise he has won, but before he can leave with the money the dark haired man will entice him back with the offer of playing for the chance of "double or nothing." The gleam in the Gambler's eye has already given him away by now, and that is when the cat and mouse shell game really starts to get interesting.

The bet is accepted and the cups are shuffled again with the fourth cup still sitting slightly off to the side, still having never been touched. The Gambler then lifts another cup and once again the bet is won and the money is paid. The dark haired man now starts to show some concern over his losing and compliments the Gambler on his uncanny ability to always find just the right cup.

The tension is high and the bet increases as the time comes to have the cups shuffled for the last time. The Gambler confident that he will win again has taken all the money he has in his pocket and laid it down for this sure to win bet. As he says, "this is all I have with me", the dark haired man just smiles back at him. The cup is lifted and the ball is missing, but to prove there really is a ball under one of the cups on the table, the dark haired man will lift the fourth cup and show you what has been hiding under it the entire time.

All the "Empty Pockets" Gambler could do now was walk away and the dark haired man then starts looking around for the next curious person who would be willing to stop and take his bet.

147

For as you see, a good Con Artist can first attract you with your curiosity; then he will work on your gullibility, vanity, pride, and last but not least your greed. A good Con Artist doesn't see the **person** in front of him, he only sees the **person**ality.

End of Story

The Power Of Persuasion

A SHORT STORY

Does this sound familiar to you? It's Monday morning and the weekend went great. All is right with the world and you are primed and ready to face the new week with what ever it might decide to bring your way. You walk into the front door of your job, punch the time clock, turn on the power to your computer and then sit down in your swivel chair just waiting for you in your own personal office. Oh yeah, I forgot to mention that you have already gone into the lounge area and fixed yourself your usual morning cup of coffee, and I have to admit, it is extra good to the last drop this fine Monday morning.

"It is going to be a Great day", is what you tell a co worker of yours named Ned when he comes to your desk and asks you how your day is going. After Ned finishes going over a few things with you, he is just about to leave your office when he stops and says, "Hey friend, you know you are looking kinda thin, are you on that "eat nothing" diet again? Of course you say no, that just isn't so, but thanks for asking."

On your way back to your office from getting another cup of that great tasting coffee, Ned stands up and says, "Hey friend, your head is hanging kinda low and you're walking sorta slow, tell me are you ill? Do you need a pill?" As you look down at your feet, you reply, "No, I don't feel ill, but if I need a pill, I'm sure you can fill the bill, but thanks for asking."

It's lunchtime and as you sit to dine, Ned looks over and asks you for the time. You raise your arm and look at your watch; it is then that Ned says, "Hey friend, are you Ok? I don't think it is right for your left arm to shake that way. Or maybe it could be you are just cold?" With a look of doubt on your face you reply, "I feel fine Ned, and once again thanks for asking.

At the end of the day, Ned couldn't help but say, "Hey friend, you really look like a mess, are you still working under a lot of stress?" Of course at that point your answer to Ned had no choice but be, "**YES**", and I really wish you would stop asking.

The next day Ned seems quite concerned when he asks your boss why you aren't at work. You shouldn't be surprised with the answer your boss will give Ned, when he tells him that you called in sick complaining of over all weakness, loss of appetite, tremors, chills and your hair seems to be falling out, possibly due to some unforeseen stress.

For as you see, I know beyond a shadow of a doubt, that if I were to question you about a freckle you have on the side of your face, I could get you to go to a mirror and look at it, and then if I were to comment about how I thought it was a little bit darker in color and somewhat less round in shape, then before the day was over, believe me when I tell you that you would be sitting at a phone trying to set up a Doctor's appointment just to get that freckle checked out by a local dermatologist. I have to admit though; the power of persuasion isn't new to mankind. It has been around a very long time and started way back with an apple in a garden. You see it wasn't temptation that got Eve in trouble; nope it wasn't temptation at all, it truly was the power of persuasion instead.

End of Story

The Year Of The Wolf

A SHORT STORY

Even though we live in a time where the wolf's presence can be seen coming from miles away, that knowledge still don't ease the suffering we all must feel.

It was time for her little man to be put to bed for the night, so as Lisa carried him upstairs with his little head resting on her shoulder, she couldn't help but thank the Good Lord for the chance to once again tuck him in for the night. Of course the second Timmy's little head hit the pillow his eyes opened wide and told his Mom that he was ready for her to read him his night-night story. Lisa could tell by the way he was yawning and rubbing his little eyes that it would only take a page or two of reading before he would once more be sound asleep. She reached for the storybook that was lying on the bedside table and asked Timmy which one of the tales that he wanted her to read to him. Timmy quickly replied, "The Three Little Pigs", as he pointed to the big bad wolf at the first little pig's doorway. Lisa said, "Ok baby, but are you sure you are not getting tired of this one and maybe want me to read you "Little Red Riding

Hood" instead?" Timmy said, "No Mommy, I want to find out what happens to the third little pig's house. I promise to stay awake this time, OK?" Lisa said, "Sure Baby", but in her heart she really didn't think he would be able to keep that promise.

With each page that she turned she would quickly glance over at her sleepy-eyed little boy to find that he was indeed still awake. The closer the wolf got to the third little pig's house, the more interested Lisa became in finding out why her Son needed to stay awake until the story ended. As she said the words "The End", Lisa smiled and hugged Timmy, before she told him goodnight. As he hugged his Mom, Timmy asked, "Mommy, when can we go home?" Lisa said, "Why baby, don't you like staying with Uncle Bill?" Timmy replied, "Sure Mommy, but I really would like to sleep in my own bed soon." Lisa had to clear the lump from her throat when she added that they would be able to go back home again soon hopefully right before the Holidays.

Timmy asked, "Mommy is the reason we can't go home because of the wind, like the wind the big bad wolf blew?" Lisa replied, "Yes, baby just like what the big bad wolf blew; only a lot more wind for a lot longer time." Timmy then thought for a moment and said, "But Mommy if our house is made out of bricks just like the third little pig built then maybe the big bad wolf wasn't able to blow it down." Lisa was just about at the point of tears when she shook her head and told Timmy that he was right, their house didn't get blown down. So then Timmy with a puzzled look on his face asked, "Mommy if it didn't get blown down then why can't we go home now?" Lisa just replied as a tear ran down her face, "Baby, this time when the wolf came it wasn't the wind that the wolf blew that made us have to leave our home, it was the flood of tears that he brought with him that made us have to leave instead."

For as you see, now can this story have a happy ending when there was so many people devastated the day the wolf came knocking on their doors.

THE FOR AS YOU SEE TALES

This story is dedicated to my loving Sister, who gave of her time and talent the summer of 2005. She volunteered more than just time; she volunteered her heart to help the multitude of people displaced by a "wolf "named Katrina.

There is no End to this Story

Will It Be Yes Or Will It Be No?

A SHORT STORY

The Mall was always packed with people shopping at lunchtime, but that never stopped Bobbie from taking her usual "walk a mile around the Mall" daily exercise. All the shops were open for noonday shoppers and all the store windows were stuffed full of bargains just waiting for someone to tell the store clerk that they were ready to pay the price showing.

Each day as she walked the mall, Bobbie would always pass by this one particular jewelry store and just for a split second she would let her eyes glance over at the window. She couldn't help herself; she just had to make sure that the ring was still sitting in the storefront window shinning brightly there for all to see. At least once a week Bobbie will go into the store after her walk and get the salesclerk to reach into the window and hand her the ring. Then she would try it on her right hand, and of course it will always fit perfectly and look like it was made just for her hand and hers alone. She will look at the ring for at least a good 5 minutes before she will

THE FOR AS YOU SEE TALES

remove it and gently hand it back to the salesclerk to be replaced back into the window.

Every now and then the salesclerk will ask her if she is ready to buy the ring or at least put it on their layaway plan and just pay for it a little bit at a time until the $200.00 note is paid for. Bobbie would just say, "I wish I could but it is a <u>want</u> and not a <u>need</u>. So I'll just have to wait. Thank you for showing it to me though. Maybe next time I'll be able to get it." The price isn't that steep, but Bobbie being a very good Mom has to put her children's needs before any of her own wishes or wants.

The end of another week came and just as she was starting her last two rounds of the walk, she looked for her ring, but it was not in the window as usual, but in the hands of a stately looking rich old man. With her ring in his hands Bobbie's heart sank, and when she rounded the corner for her last leg of the walk she saw that the man and her ring was gone. Her steps slowed down as she tried to finish her walk even though she knew in her heart that the ring she had wanted for months and months was now gone.

Still it wasn't until she finished her walk that she allowed herself to stop at the store to find out about what had happened to the ring, besides what was the point, the ring was nowhere in sight.

The look of sorrow and dread was all over Bobbie's face as she asked her new found friend behind the counter, if the man who had just left had purchased the ring. The clerk said, "I thought you really wanted that ring, so when that man told me he wanted to get it for his wife, I found myself letting out a deep sigh of relief when he handed it back to me and said that he would return tomorrow with his wife to decide, and so I set the ring out of sight right here under my counter."

It was at that time that the salesclerk reached under the counter and pulled out the ring and then handed it over to Bobbie. As she placed the ring on her finger she told the clerk **thank you** so many times that the clerk had to stop her just so she could get a word in edgewise. The clerk reminded Bobbie that if she didn't do something about the ring that the man said he would be coming back in tomorrow with his wife. Bobbie told the clerk that she would find the money it would take to get the ring, even if she had to get two part time jobs, one for herself and one for the clerk. The clerk just laughed, and told her that this was a part time job for her, but that she agreed that she should find a way to get the ring for herself.

It took more than 5 minutes before the clerk could get the ring back from Bobbie; in fact, it was more than just a little past closing time before the ring was placed safely away for the night.

For as you see, If you procrastinate long enough don't be surprised when you reach out for what you want, just to find out, it isn't there any longer and you have to come back empty handed.

End of Story

Workmanship

A SHORT STORY

It is mid November at my house and time for my annual "what will I buy everyone for Christmas dilemma stress test". This year there will be a whole lot less stress on me, simply because I am going to downsize my list of family I am going to buy for. That may sound mean, but it is what I must do if I plan on keeping my sanity throughout the up and coming shopping season. Christmas is such a trying time of year for me. My family and friends know exactly what I am talking about when I say, "Christmas bah humbug", and so without further ado, now on with my story.

The week in between Christmas and New Years is always the busiest time of year for our local department store. That is you know because everyone in town is coming in just to exchange their Christmas presents they received from Cousin Fred or Aunt Jane, for something that they really had wanted all along. This year the return line seemed exceptionally long and slow. So while waiting in the return line about ¾ of the way back, Jack opened the sack he had brought with him. In it was the watch that his Mom had given him; the one he now was being forced to bring back to the store for an exchange. The watch was a nice present, don't get me wrong, it just didn't run but for about 24 hrs before the battery would give out and then it would slowly lose time until eventually the hands of the watch stopped moving completely. Jack had already gone through two new watch batteries in a valiant effort to try and make his present work properly, but with the two earlier attempts both ending in failure; Jack had no choice but to fight the crowd and stand in line while waiting his turn in the "Slower than Christmas" "After Christmas Returns Line".

No man in his right mind would stand still the whole length of time it was going to take to try and return anything after Christmas, but since Jack wasn't married he had no other choice, so there he stood. It didn't take but about an hour before Jack started noticing that most of the presents that everyone was returning in front of him seemed to be all about the same size, and of course it didn't take a Rocket Scientist like Jack very long before he noticed that about every other return was a watch that looked very similar to his own.

Curiosity mixed with boredom took over and Jack decided to ask a couple of women in front of him if they too were exchanging a watch. He was and at the same time wasn't shocked to find out that about three more exchanges around him were watches also. Every one of the watches being exchanged seemed to be plagued with the same defect. It was at that point that Jack decided he needed to get his money back instead of risking a replacement watch with the same inherent flaw built in.

As Jack stepped up to the counter and placed his watch down the Clerk didn't even ask what was wrong with his watch, instead he just gave Jack his money back, no questions asked.

For as you see, there is a good reason why antiques are a lot more costly, if not priceless to buy. One of the most obvious reasons is because of the "hands on" Workmanship that went into the construction of each and every piece. Then there is also another good reason for antiques to cost more and that is because they were

THE FOR AS YOU SEE TALES

made to last and not just made out of particle board that comes apart with the least little drop of water that it comes it contact with.

The bottom line is, you get what you pay for, but in today's times, even with name brand products that you once could trust and love to use over and over again; you really can't trust them anymore because most of them now send that same product overseas to be built by other countries just because of the cheaper labor cost.

You know as well as I do that nothing coming off the production line today will be built to last, instead it will only be priced a little bit cheaper in the hope that when you do have to buy another one then maybe you will be able to afford the replacement you will need to buy next year at this time. What a waste of time shopping and total lack of Workmanship from my point of view.

End of Story

I'm Covered

A SHORT STORY

There are certain laws of nature that are real, but can not be easily explained or understood. Take for instance the ever present "Law of Gravity". How many of you sitting there can explain to me how the "Law of Gravity" works to keep you in your seat? Well if you are like me, then the answer to that question is "not many" and if I were to venture so far as to ask how many of you sitting there could explain to me the "Law of Murphy" (or better known to some as "Murphy's Law") what do you think that answer would be? Probably about the same response as I received to my first question – not many. Well for the very few of you that have never heard of, or experienced "Murphy Law" let me take a few moments to enlighten you. "Murphy's Law" broadly states that "**Whatever can go wrong will go wrong**". With that said and before I start to get as boring to you as your last science Professor, I find it time to get on with my story.

You know there is nothing as exciting as a well planed vacation and skiing each year with the boys, was the only thing Murphy and

THE FOR AS YOU SEE TALES

Mat talked about at their "every Friday night card game". Playing Poker once a week kept the group of five happily married men united and at the same time out of trouble and harms way sitting at one or the others kitchen table to the wee hours of the morning. Their wives didn't mind of course because if you think about it, it was only one Friday out of five and the hand the Ladies got dealt was one of unlimited every Saturday morning shopping with their husbands having to recoup on the couch and watch TV with the kids. Of course the only ones watching the cartoons were the kids, while their Dads just watched the back of their eyelids.

Steamboat Springs, Colorado was this year's pick of Ski Resorts for the boy's yearly vacation get away, and Murphy was the first one to ask if they all were packed and ready to leave for the plane the next morning. Mat of course was joking when he said he wasn't going to pack until it was almost time to leave, because truthfully he had been packed for at least a month now.

It was Murphy's turn to shuffle the cards and deal when he reminded everyone that they needed to double check and make sure they hadn't forgotten to pack all their paperwork like insurance cards, money, and airline tickets.

That's when Mat said, "but Murphy why should I bring my insurance cards?" Murphy replied, "Mat what are you going to do if you get sick while we are away?" Mat said "well that is a good point old friend". The question of insurance by Mat started Murphy to have doubts as to other problems that might arise that Mat hadn't thought about; so Murphy posed the question to Mat, "hey Mat did you happen to remember to purchase any travelers insurance just in case you have to cancel and not go on this vacation for one reason or another?" Mat quickly relied, "no, I do not think I did. I guess now would be just a little bit too late to try and get some, since our flight will be leaving in about 6 hours from now. Oh well, maybe I'll remember to get some next year. By the way, whose turn is it to deal anyway?" Murphy jokingly replied, "Leave it up to you and this game won't be over until we get back from Colorado."

The clock struck 3 AM and past time for the boys to call it a night. Just as Mat was turning to go out the front door, he was too busy counting his winning to notice the thin sheet of ice that had formed covering the entrance steps and walkway of Murphy's suburban home. Just one step forward and Mat's feet came right out from under him, and he landed on his right wrist and knee. As he lay there waiting for his friends to call 911, all he could say in-between moans was "Murphy please tell me that your homeowners' insurance is up to date, because we are going to need it." Murphy reassuringly replied, "That's what friends and insurances are for."

For as you see, You know, I would be more than willing to bet you that even before the first car started rolling off the production line that someone who knew of Murphy's Law was standing there with a pen and paper in his hand taking notes writing

"please send out a memo, I think there maybe a need for someone to invent automobile insurance", and if I were a really smart cookie, I would come up with an insurance to protect all the good drivers, who drive and obey the speed limit, from the ones who feel the burning need to pass them by. I think I'll name this insurance after one of the speeding driver's front seat passengers. I'll call it **"ROAD RAGE INSURANCE"**. All because of Murphy and his law a new Insurance is born.

End of Story

One Last Dance

A SHORT STORY

If you had the chance to do it all again, knowing what the outcome would be, would you still take the chance and just do it? The answer to that question can only be answered by the individual taking that journey, but my answer to that question will always be "yes". For as you see, I am a risk taker.

Oh, to be young again, to be standing in the shadows of your one and only Senior Prom. Being the biggest of wall flowers, I wasn't asked out to the prom, but neither was my best friend Shelly. She pushed me and pushed me until I went shopping with her at our favorite mall store, and then she helped me pick out the flashiest pink satin dress the store had to offer, and then of course I had to buy one that was one size too small. No one but me would have done that with just a pipe dream hope that I could lose enough weight in the one month it would take to pull that dress up over my thighs, which was of course all the time I had left before the prom was to begin. At school anytime I wanted to eat a candy bar Shelly would just stare me down until I would let go of the death grip that I had on my favorite lunch desert. When the time came somehow she managed to stuff me into that dress and somehow she got me into our high school gym just as the prom music started playing.

The first boy that came into the gym unescorted came over and asked Shelly to dance, which was no surprise to anyone who knew her. Hours and dances went by and still no one had dared to ask me to dance. I was just about to chalk this prom off as a total loss, when out of the corner of my eye I spied Tom coming from across the other side of the room headed right in my direction. He was one of the less popular guys at school and most of the time I wouldn't have said one word to him, but for some reason he really looked much taller in his new prom suit. Blame it on the music, blame it on the lighting, or just blame it on the night, but I swear the closer he came to me the more handsome he became.

As the next to last dance started we began swaying with the music, and like a magnet attracting opposites, I felt him starting to pull me in closer and closer to him. I swear there was something about his cologne that made me slowly lay my head on his shoulder, and then with my eyes closed I found myself wishing the music would never stop. When the last dance was over and the night was at an end, I bet you can't guess what happened next. Well, maybe I was wrong, maybe you can guess that he asked my out the very next weekend and of course I said "yes".

For as you see, nothing taste better than that last piece of pie, nothing feels better than your last kiss, and no memory is more lasting to you than that last dance of the night.

End of Story

The Right Move

A SHORT STORY

It was just about coming down to the wire. At the start of the first round of eliminations more than two thousand contestants had shown up to try and win the title of Grand Chess Master. The event covered all the ends of the globe and the rules were simple, the player who won the first two out of three games in a match ending in checkmate would then move on to the next table until only two players would be remaining to play the final set of games.

To the left hand side of the table sat the youngest player who was from Russia, and on the right hand side sat the older player from Staten Island, New York. The Grand Finals started as all the other games had before it, always with the first move being made by the player sitting to the right hand side of the table. Since they had both gotten this far in the contest the Judges knew the two remaining players would be the best in the world, and for that they earned the respect they deserved from the on looking crowd as well as the seated panel of judges.

Midday and the finals had commenced. You had to really have been paying close attention to the board and its chess pieces to have seen the move the player from New York had made. Even I wasn't quit sure he had even made a move, that is, until I watched the instant replay on my TV set. So then the next move came with it being Russia's turn. I had watched enough of Russia's previous matches to know that time really didn't mean that much to him, so it didn't surprise me to find him still sitting there contemplating his opening move even after I had gone to the kitchen to make myself a sandwich, poured myself a drink of tea, and then grabbed a bag of chips to eat.

It was no surprise still, to find out that after I had finished eating and returned to my living room and reclined back that he still hadn't decided which move he wanted to make. Finally about a half hour later it was New York's turn again and just as quickly as he had made the first move, bam, he made his second and was done.

Each time the game was declared a stalemate and the game had to be restarted. The New York player got faster with his moves and Russia player took longer and longer to decide. After the second full day of finals and the hopes of either player ever getting a checkmate on the other faded; it became painfully obvious a decision had to be made as to who really was the winner and that call was totally left in the hands of the panel of ten Judges. I expected it to take a while for the ruling, but that wasn't the case at all, and just as the announcer said, "And the winner by unanimous decision is......." my cable went out.

Now don't sit there and try to tell me you do not know who the Judges picked as the winner, you know as well as I do that they picked the one who showed them the most confidence with the quickest most deliberate moves know to man.

For as you see, confidence in yourself can be the only thing that will make you stand out in a crowd and when that crowd happens to all be applying for the same job then maybe that little bit of added confidence in what you do, just might end up paying off for you. FYI, just so you know, with confidence, no **right move** has ever had to be questioned.

End of Story

All In The Name Of The King

A SHORT STORY

As this story goes, it was a time of Kings and Kingdoms, so as we start this story try to envision if you will, the King proudly sitting on his throne, in his fortress of a castle, being surrounded by all his beloved followers. Everyone before him loved their King and as with all his beloved peasants, each and every one of them would gladly give up their lives in order to protect their King. As the King spoke, the room became quite with all standing there waiting anxiously to hear what news the King had to declare for them this week. Not even his closest confidants could have been prepared for what the King was now ready to proclaim to them.

As he started to speak, the first thing on his agenda was, "The State of the Kingdom Report". In the report the King stated that no other country around his Kingdom would ever be able to match the fire power that he had built up in the Army that guarded him, and because of his Army's strength there would no longer be a need for any of the peasants to keep their own personal weapons. So a decree would be written that within a week all weapons would be confiscated (all in the name of the King). The roar of agreement from all there rang out through the castle halls, like the sound you would expect to hear coming from the castle's tower bell at dinnertime.

David's village lies on the outer regions of the King's Kingdom, and so the week was just about over before the word of the King's decree finally reached his house. David being the best blacksmith in the Kingdom, and one of the Kings devoted followers couldn't help but be a little bit upset at having his only livelihood taken away from him, but the word of the King was the law. Of course, you should be told that David is the only person around with the talent it takes to make the finest weapons that the King would now be demanding, but still a decree from the King should never be taken lightly.

When the guards came, David instantly handed over his swords, knives, bows and arrows without even a single harsh word being spoken. Everyone in the village quickly obeyed the King, but it seemed like less than a week had passed before another decree reached the village, and this time the guards would be coming to confiscate all the pitchforks and machetes in the Kingdom as well. As David handed over what the King had decreed to be taken from him; he stopped just long enough to ask the guard why the King had felt the need to take all their tools for working in their fields, and once again as the guard had done in the past he quoted from the decree that the King's army was strong enough to protect everyone in the Kingdom so there wouldn't be any need for personal sharp objects of any kind. After the guard left the village David called all his friends and family together into his barn for their weekly town meeting. It wasn't but about 20 minutes before the King's guard returned and stated that next week the King would be wanting all of them to turn over any clubs and/or bats that they might have, and that the only reason he didn't take them with him at this time was because the King's cart wasn't big enough to carry all of the confiscated items at one time.

THE FOR AS YOU SEE TALES

As the guard turned to leave David had just one question to ask of him. As David's voice started to quiver he asked, "How long will it take the King's army to come to our village if ever we find a need for them to defend us?" There was a dead silence in the room as the guard replied, "You know, I'll just have to get back with you next week about this matter, but be assured I'll have an answer for you when I return", and as he turned and drove the cart away you could hear the back and forth rattling of the machetes and pitchforks as the village's last line of defense left for the castle neatly stacked up to the top rim of the King's cart.

Even without the use of modern day electricity, you could see the light bulbs turning on, one by one, inside the heads of all the people standing in David's barn that night, and needless to say the very next day, almost before day break there was an assembly line of people gathering outside David's barn door just to help him get his workday started. So as you have already guessed, before that day was over everyone in the village suddenly became a certified blacksmith.

For as you see, as a child we would always say, "sticks and stones may break my bones, but words will never hurt me", but as an adult I have come to find that childhood saying isn't entirely true if the word "confiscate" can be used to leave you defenseless one day with nothing but "sticks and stones" left around to throw at your enemies. I just hope that one day I do not have to suddenly become a blacksmith myself just so I can have a metal object in my hands to use as protection when push comes to shove.

End of Story

Change

A SHORT VISION

When Jonas exited the boat exhausted from making the long journey back to his hometown, he wasn't sure exactly how he would be able to find his way around. In the back of his mind he could still see every street corner and every storefront window decked out with gifts he wanted for Christmas that year, but all of those images were from a time long past. Surely time must have changed the place he once called home, but to his joy and surprise it seemed like time hadn't managed to change anything at all. Every tree and house he remembered was still all neatly lined up down Main Street, and as he walked toward his old neighborhood; Jonas couldn't help but feel the excitement start to grow in anticipation of getting to visit with all his old friends.

In the middle of all the excitement Jonas forgot to look both ways as he stepped out into the street on his way over to the old country store. All he had on his mind at the time was how good the milkshakes had tasted there and how hot it was outside at the moment. Jonas's eyes opened wide when he felt the pain coming from his right ankle and it took more than a few seconds before he realized that he had awoken lying in a hospital bed located in the emergency room of the old charity hospital. The look on his face showed how frightened and hurt he really was, and even though his injuries were minor, the pain Jonas felt was more than what he could or wanted to handle at the moment; so Jonas asked the first nurse he saw if he could talk to a Doctor and all she said was that the Doctor would be there soon. It was almost an hour later before Jonas was able to stop the nurse and ask her why the ER Doctor hadn't come into see him and could he get something for all his pain. He then added that he thought his ankle was broken from the way it looked and felt. The nurse once again stalled and answered Jonas's question with the same answer as before, but this time he could sense more than just a little bit of impatience in her voice as she told him, "The Doctor will be with you soon."

Well you guessed it; another hour passed and still nothing for his pain, no Doctor and no x-rays. Finally frantic, Jonas demanded his nurse to tell him just exactly what was taking them so long. It was then that she finally explained away the delay by saying, "You know we still live in the dark ages, and in this small town nothing ever seems to change. Doctor Jones remember still has to cross two mountains just to get here and with good weather like today he should be here in about another 30 minutes." Jonas said, "Doctor Jones, do you mean old Doctor Fred Jones, the same country Doctor that delivered me 30 years ago, that Doctor Fred Jones?" The nurse laughed as she said, "Well I guess you already know one another, don't you?" Jonas wasn't smiling as his face started to turn a pale green, and he asked her for a basin as she handed it to him he told her to add something else to his current list of complaints, because now that she had given him that news, he was starting to feel really sick at his stomach.

For as you see, some things have to change in order to stay current. Medicine is one of those things, and if you would like to know what I see happening in my future of medicine then please read on; because one day there will not be any paper trail once you enter the hospital, no nurse will ever get writer's cramps in their fingers, medical records will be a thing of the past, and one day your total stay will be a total virtual reality tour caught on tape.

Your stay will be stored away sort of like what you see from the dashboard of one of the local patrol cars that now videos your every move at all routine traffic stops. Each nurse will have their very own personal daily log cam which is something similar to a Spy Cam combined with a Nanny Cam, it will be attached to their ID badges and record what they do for you from the time they clock in until the time they go home. All medicines they give you will be scanned visually by the pharmacist and if it is the wrong meds or the wrong patient then the bottle will automatically have the cap lock down and only a pharmacist will be able to unlock it.

Also one day you will be able to go to any store and walk through a total body scanner that records every part of your anatomy onto a credit card size CD-MD file, and then you can take that disk to the Doctor of your choosing. The scan will tell them your past, present, and future bodily functions analysis on every organ of your body, it will also note any problems you will need to address now and in the years to come, point out points of stress, wear and tear. Oh yeah, I forgot the best part, the X-Ray Diagnostic Examiner CD will only cost you a quarter to buy.

It has always been known that if man can imagine something then it is not beyond his reach. A great example is the first step man made on the moon, which first was imagined in a cartoon and a silent movie with a man riding on the back of a rocket ship. So my question to you is, "**Why not change**, for the better or for the worse, **Why not just give change a chance**?" I did...

End of Story

Sermon On The Mountain

A SHORT STORY

Once there was a man who lived at the base of a mountain. He loved living in the woods with his yard filled with all the flowers and trees that grew there. The peacefulness of his surrounding filled his heart with joy. One day up on the mountain pretty close to the top rang out a noise. It sounded like the blast coming from a high powered shot gun. The man was sure that he heard a hunter hunting on the side of his mountain.

The man really didn't own the mountain but since he had been the only man around for miles then he had grown to claim it as his own so up the mountain the man went to see who was doing all the shooting and making all the noise. To the man's surprise he came across a well kept cabin at the top of the mountain and sitting on the front porch was an elderly old man. The young man asked, "Sir I heard a noise that sounded like shooting coming from up here, did you hear them too?" The old man said, "Sure did and I want you to know that I think I got him."

The young man looked around and didn't see a thing lying on the ground so he asked the old man exactly what he had shot at. Was it a deer, was it a bobcat, or was it a bear? The old man replied, "No siree bob, what I shot at was bigger than that." Still while looking around, the young man remarked that he saw nothing, and if the old man had gotten what he had shot at, then why wasn't he out there skinning it instead of sitting on his porch rocking with his shot gun in his lap.

That was when the old man smiled and said, "Son I would be skinning it if the Devil wasn't faster than the bullets I sent his way. Then the old man laughed when he added, and I am pretty sure I will get him on the next go round.

For as you see, We are all GOD's children. When you walk with GOD and decide to let go of his hand, whose hand do you think will be outstretched and waiting for you to hold onto. You can't walk life's path with GOD, and then walk that same path with the devil at your side. They do not go in the same direction; you have to choose which one you go through life's journey with. I just hope you choose wisely.

End of Story

Chopping Down A Cherry Tree

A SHORT STORY

If you received a new hatchet for Christmas what do you think a young boy like George would go outside and start trying to do? You guessed it; he started trying to take down trees with his new present. The first tree that he got to was as big around as he was, but that didn't stop him. He hacked and hacked until his arms got tired so he had to stop and take a little break. Since that tree was a little bit too big around for him to cut down in just one day he would have to set his sights on another one. After Christmas was over he knew the hatchet would be used only for work and not for play anymore.

He looked around and he saw a very tall tree, but it wasn't that big around. As he drew back the hatchet it dawned on him that even though he could take the tree down that maybe it might not fall in the direction that he intended it to fall. What if it landed on his house? So he let the hatchet go back down to his side without hitting the tall tree with it.

There was only one more tree in his front yard that was left to tackle. It just happened to be a cherry tree. Even though this would be the first year it bore fruit it wasn't until George saw the bright red cherries hanging from its branches did he know what kind of tree it really was. In two whacks of the hatchets down came the tree, even George was amazed at how easy the tree was to cut down.

Out the front door Mary Ball (his Mother) came running over to her tree lying there in front of her. She was almost in tears, and could have administered corporal punishment, but she knew of a better way to teach her young son a lesson. His wise Mom just pointed to the tree, and told George that this year for his birthday he was not going to get his favorite cherry pie.

George was devastated. Every year he had asked his Mom for a cherry pie instead of a birthday cake for his birthday, and every year she would have to go to the neighbor's house and buy enough cherries just to make his pie with.

Mary said," George because of your actions you will have to go and plant me another cherry tree, and then wait until it bears fruit before I will make you another cherry pie for your birthday." All George could say was "yes ma'am".

For as you see, I bet if you look at the trees planted on the first white house grounds you will find that there was a cheery tree planted there in the bunch. If you look at the white house grounds today, and don't see a cherry tree; I would just be curious as to **who** cut down George Washington's cherry tree?

I would be willing to bet that George T. will be given the blame for that missing tree. What do you bet?

HaHaHa

End of Story

You Take The High Road And I'll Take The Low Road

A SHORT STORY

Everyone knows that the "pot of gold" at the end of the rainbow belongs to the Leprechauns. By definition a Leprechaun is a type of fairy of the Aos Sí in Irish folklore. So since I am Scotch Irish I have looked for that pot of gold every time a rainbow appears before me. If you believe in Leprechauns do you know how they came to own all that gold? Well this is where my story will help you answer that question.

It starts off by introducing you to Scotty and Blarney. They were the two best gold thieves in the county. Little by little, night after night, the two of them would sneak past the guards up in the guard tower in front of the company's gold mine. At first the little thieves got away with the company's gold sneaking past the guards with gold sticking out of their pockets. It wasn't long before the company started noticing their losses as the pile of gold never seemed to be getting any higher, even though their work crew employees were steadily making the pile higher at the end of their shifts each day.

Something was a miss so the company set up cameras, and the first night they caught the two little green guys waddling out of the cave with their pants almost coming down to their knees. It was decided by the company to set up a trap and catch Scotty and Blarney red handed in the act of stealing their gold.

As the light shone down on the two from the guard's flashlights; all you saw was a flash of green as the two flew the entrance to the cave. The gold fell out of their pockets leaving a bright shinny trail right to the two hiding out up a tree. After being taken off to

Jail, Scotty sat on the jail cell bench and asked Blarney, "What do we do now?" Blarney said, "Empty out your pockets." Then he let out a big chuckle. So they emptied out the remaining gold from their pockets, and then sat off in the corner just waiting until the light of day shone threw the window of their jail cell.

It didn't take long before the jailor came to the jail cell door in order to check in on them. Where are you two? is all the jailor could say when he found the cell empty with only a pile of gold lying in the middle of the jail cell floor. Well of course when the cell door opened the two Leprechauns just quietly walked out of the open door, and walked away to go steal another day.

When Scotty was sure no one could hear him he stopped and asked Blarney, "Why did we have to leave the gold behind Blarney?" Scotty reminded him that even though they couldn't be seen by day; the moon dust used to make gold invisible hadn't been field tested yet, but once it passed inspection then they all would be rich.

For as you see, the light of day makes Leprechauns, like all the other fairies invisible. But at night with a flashlight you might get a glimpse of one running away from you with his pockets full of your Gold.

End of Story

For Lauren

CHAPTER FOUR

For My Eyes Only

A Little Known Fact About Gnomes

A Short Story

It depends on what you believe in, as to whether or not you believe in Gnomes, and since I believe in all kinds of fabled beings, then it only stands to reason that I would also tend to believe in Gnomes. As per already known description a Gnome is a fabled race of diminutive subterranean beings, guardians of mines, quarries, etc. The image of a Gnome is a very popular one, and used often as a yard ornament, but did you know that they also like to fish and are so very tight with their money so tight that they squeak when they walk. Well up until this last week, I had never actually seen one, then the phone rang and all that changed.

I decided to sell my aluminum boat to help supplement the cost of purchasing my up and coming book that has now gone on sell with my publicist on the internet. After the advertisement came out I had several people come out to look at the boat, but for one reason or another the boat just didn't fit their needs, and so Wednesday

THE FOR AS YOU SEE TALES

night a little after 10 PM a call came in. Half awake I answered the phone and at first I thought I was talking to a little old lady (I did have the age right but by no means was he a lady or a gentleman for that matter). He would ask me a question, then I would ask him one, and of course all that time I was trying to determine his gender without actually coming out and being completely rude. Just when I was pretty certain that the person I was talking to was this very feisty little old woman, I asked her what she was going to do with the boat, since even at my age the boat would be too much for me to handle alone. He quickly let me know that it was none of my business as to what the boat was going to be used for, it was just my business to sell it, and that he was a man and by no means a woman.

I told him that if he had of just given me his name then I would have known that he was a man. That was when he sharply told me that I hadn't asked. I started to hang up at that point, but something told me that the person I was talking to was a real and true to life Gnome.

The longer we talked the more interested in him I became so I quickly got to the point where I just wanted to meet the little man, behind the little voice. After he hung up the phone and the meeting was set; he let me get just about back to sleep before he called me back, and I truly believe he called me back just to get back at me for mistakenly calling him a "feisty little old woman".

Well, it was official the search for the little Gnome was on. I gave him directions to my house and made wagers at work as to what he would look like. He had already let me know that he was 76, and very capable of handling my 16-foot boat and trailer, and as a matter of fact that would be all he would let me know. When he showed up that Friday evening the first thing he said as he exited his truck was that he could see at least 5 cracks in the boat's hull from where he was standing 5 feet away. I know my mouth had to have gone through the motions without actually verbalizing "GNOME" as I stood there staring at him. The little man was old but could still get around pretty good except for a visible leaning to his right side as he walked, and upon standing up he came to just about my armpit in height. Believe me when I tell you that I have seen all kinds of short people in my lifetime, especially where I work, but this honestly was my very first Gnome, and this little Gnome really took the cake. He offered me $400.00 for a boat that was well worth about $600.00 and when I said I would let him have it for $500.00 he just told me that he would call me back at the end of the week when I was ready for him to take the boat off my hands. I said I would think about it and if he would like to leave me his name and number I would call him back.

Of course to this day I do not know either his name or his phone number, and I truly believe that if he had given me his name it probably would have been something like, Sam, or one of his other friends, of that I am certain.

For as you see, I will probably meet another Gnome in my lifetime, but there is one thing you can lay odds on, I won't ever sell a boat of mine to a little feisty old Gnome for pennies on the dollar and the boat he expects to take off my hands at the end of this week is already out of his reach.

End of Story

Being Human

A True Story

It all came about when I was 27 years of age and decided I wanted to have a Tubial Ligation surgery, just so I didn't have to take birth control pills any longer. After a couple of miscarriages, and two D & C's that followed, I decided having kids was for the birds, so Kelly and I opted for the Tubial. There wasn't anyway Kelly would go to have a vasectomy, he can't stand the sight of blood. Kelly has two girls from his first wife but he had always wanted a little boy. I told him that unless he could talk me out of it, then we would adopt a little boy if he really wanted one that badly.

The arrangements were made and the surgery scheduled for a laparoscopic tubial to be done. I arranged the week off from work and expected a hospital stay of only a day or two at the most. I checked into the hospital and I was watching TV the night before the surgery when about 10PM my nurse called me to the nurse's station and said my Doctor needed to talk to me. He told me that his Father had just died and since he couldn't do the surgery did I want to leave the hospital and reschedule my surgery **OR** would it be OK for his partner to do my surgery in the morning. I asked him if his partner would do the same surgery that he had said he was going to do with just a bikini cut and a laparoscope. My Doctor reassured me that he would, so since my job was already letting me off from work I said I wanted to go ahead with the surgery.

My nurse brought in the consent form for me to sign for the surgery and then gave me my premeds. While waiting in the surgery holding room, my surgeon introduced himself for the first time to me and only 2 minutes before I was put under anesthesia for the operation. That was the last time I saw him and to this day I still do not remember his name. When I woke up, I noticed that my scare wasn't at the bikini line on just the right side, oh NO, it was about 6" long and straight down the middle of my stomach just under my bellybutton. Since I had had previous surgery and didn't have but <u>one tube</u> that needed to be cut, my scare wasn't suppose to be but about 1" long and only on the right side. I can only imagine the look on that man's face when he looked inside me and didn't find a left sided tube to cut.

I had a different Doctor make surgical rounds everyday after my surgery, but it wasn't until the third day when it was time to remove my dressing and steristrips, that the real fun began. Come to find out I am Allergic to steristrips. The new Doctor couldn't hide the shocked look on his face when he saw the water blisters that the steristrips had formed. The steristrips were sitting on top of about a 1" high, filled with water, blister ever spot on me that the steristrips touched. He had to remove the steristrips and to do that he had to bust all the blisters, one at a time. The only good thing about it was that I didn't feel a thing when he removed the steristrips, but the blisters left more of a scar than the surgical cut did. It literally looked like a railroad track, with one long train track and then multiple steristrip crossties lying across it. Since I never saw the man again I couldn't ask him any questions and since I had signed a consent form that said Laparotomy instead of Laparoscopy, I had no one but myself to blame. It was a long time before I left the hospital and it cost me a lot more time off from work.

THE FOR AS YOU SEE TALES

For as you see, even with my working in the medical field, human errors can and will be made. Doctors are human too, and with fate at the wheel the next time I go into the hospital it might be for a Lobectomy of the lung and end up being a Lobotomy of the brain. Of course a little brain surgery might really do me some good.

End of Story

Closing Out The Account

A SHORT STORY

All we can hope for at the end of our days is to leave this life with enough money in our bank account to cover the expense that someone will have to pay just to put us to rest. I was really fortunate that both of my parents ended up leaving enough money behind to cover that expense, with just a little bit left over to go on a really nice snowmobile vacation to Jackson, WY with my Sister and my Husband.

The cost of being born has kept up with the cost of getting a divorce as well as the cost of being buried. The Hospital and your Doctor wants their money "up front", the Lawyer wants his retainer fee money "up front" and the Funeral Home wants to know how their bill will be paid "up front". This isn't anything to get upset about; it is just the American way of life.

I just wonder exactly when it became necessary to charge you for life and death. Once upon a time you could come into this world in your Mom's own bed and then when the time came you would be placed in the ground free of charge. Some people would be buried at sea wrapped in a sheet if that were where they were at their time of death. Some people like the Vikings would be set a blaze and go up in a fiery flame of glory, while others like the American Indians would be elevated up off the ground just to keep down the animal attacks and then free their spirits to the four winds. I think the cost may have started with the need for embalming. The Egyptians must have been the first ones to have paid a King's ransom for their embalming and in turn try to clinch the promise of life after death.

I, for one believe in life after death, but contrary to most beliefs, I also believe in reincarnation and have had many past lives of my own. One day if you would like to talk more on the subject just look me up, I'm not really sure exactly what my name will be at that time or how old I will be, but I know if you ask me I'll be able to answer any question you might have to send my way. Believe me, I know exactly how strange this sounds to you, so because of my out of the ordinary thinking this will be as far as I will go on the subject of reincarnation at this time, now back to my story.

When my Parents died, my Dad on "1/26/84" and my Mom on "8/21/03", I being the oldest was chosen to handle all the final finances (to close the accounts) I guess you could say. Something I did quite well, I might add. Was it an easy thing to do? Not by any means, but even if it is a dirty job "Someone has to do it." With my handling all the affairs of the estate, the burden was then lifted from my Brothers and Sister. Would I have chosen not to be the one to lean on? The answer to that is certainly not, because "that is what Tiggers do best." All of this sounds like it comes straight from my stories, well you are right, and most of my strength to get through the hard times has come from my stories. For that I am grateful that the passion for my writing is there to help me along the path I have to follow.

For as you see, we have to do what we have to do in life, just try and make your parents proud of you in life as well as in death.

End of Story

Cry Me A River

A SHORT STORY

If every person on this earth would cry a few tears all at the same time, then all of us would drown from the flood that would follow. As the world's population expands, the land we stand on shrinks from global warming. The simple fact is that global warming is causing the polar ice caps to melt, which in turn, covers even more of the land we need to stand on. Where is this all leading to, God only knows, but from where I stand the future of mankind isn't looking all that great.

The only thing that gives me hope for our future is the fact that the Bible says God has promised not to destroy the world again with water, and with that promise he gave us his rainbow as a reminder every time it rains. Man has built dams to hold back the rivers, he has built towers to predict the storms, but he hasn't done anything to rebuild the ozone layer which protects us from solar rays and global warming. Man can transform almost any gas on earth into a useful product and then exploit it for their own gain. So why can't

THE FOR AS YOU SEE TALES

man add more of the ozone gases back into the ozone layer and stop its deterioration from coming to the breaking point of no return?

Just take and reinject the planets outer shell with gases, kinda of like when you reinflate a flat tire, one gas at a time. To clean the ozone maybe we will have to give it a bath, or maybe we will have to recirculate it through one big filtering system, I do not know what it will take, but if anyone would ask me, then I know I could come up with more of a suggestion box, than most scientist have done to this date. If we can send a rocket ship through the ozone layer on its way into outer space then why can't this same ship dump some needed ozone gases out of its tanks as they pass from layer to layer? It may be just as simple as floating an orbital watering station like a sprinkler system orbiting the earth and setting it to go off at different rotations around the planet, with scheduled times to refill the tanks from water pumped straight from the ocean floor. Sounds good to me, and so why can't that work?

For as you see, a rocket scientist, I am not, but I do know that if something isn't done pretty soon, then acid rain will be just small fish to fry compared to the heat that global warming is starting to generate.

End of Story

Defining Crazy

MY PERCEPTION

I've often wondered if the way I see my world doesn't borderline on insanity. So to ease my mind, I decided to define what I have found to be just a little bit over the edge of reason, or as some would like to refer to as being just a wee bit *crazy*. See if you don't find yourself concurring (sorry just a little Doc humor).

Examples of Crazy:

As an adult you work hard to afford a big house with a whole lot of rooms, but in the end you are placed in a nursing home with just two twin beds in a space no bigger than your average jail cell.

You try desperately to keep a clean house when there is nothing but dirt all around you.

Always finding yourself taking the blame for events that are totally out of your control.

Constantly worrying yourself into extreme obesity.

Living your life as if you are on a short leash.

Closing your door to family, no matter what they have done to you.

THE FOR AS YOU SEE TALES

Keeping secrets from someone, and then asking for their help in the same breath.

Working day after day with no actual goal in mind.

Thinking you can stay ahead of the rising cost of living, and last but not least always being a pessimistic person who can never find a reason to smile.

For as you see, call me crazy, if you will, but I see all the afore mentioned quirks in just about everyone around me. So is the whole world crazy? <u>Well it takes one to know one,</u> they say.

End of Story

From A Frog To A Prince

A SHORT STORY

At first glance I would have to say, it looked like just another very old, well-used piece of junk. One you would find any day of the week just lying around really close to the edge of the road patiently waiting for the garbage truck to come along and haul it off to the nearest landfill location. Not true for my Sister though, because unlike me, it didn't take but a fraction of a second's glance at it for her to fall madly in love.

It was a wonderful day, and the anticipation of going to Canton, Texas would always make us get up extra early on the first Saturday of each month in spring and fall. The weather was bright and sunny, and the wild flowers were just starting to show their little heads up along I-20 as we rode off in search of a treasured find at Canton's flea market place. On this quest Kelly would be going for his usual purchase of work gloves, dozens at a time, while Bobbie, my Sister, professed she would be looking for an antique claw foot tub, and I of course needed anything that suited my fancy and pocket book. Bobbie, I call her Beanie for short, claimed she was only looking for

THE FOR AS YOU SEE TALES

a tub right now and that she wasn't going to buy one at this time. Yeah Right! As soon as she hit the front entrance to Canton her claw foot tub feelers rose right out of the top of her head and she started up her claw foot tub radar scanner. Beanie started sweeping the whole area just like a treasure hunter would sweep the ground in search of a well-hidden pot of gold. It was slim pickens this weekend for antique tubs, and so without one in sight she had to resort to asking everyone she met if they had seen a vendor with one for sell, it just so happened that the second person she asked had one for sell right in the back of his nearby pickup truck.

My Sister's eyes lit up to the point that when she looked into the bed of his truck you would have sworn it was midnight and she had the only flashlights beaming around for miles. The vendor couldn't help but see how much my Sister really wanted that tub. Her gemmy gemmy eyes and visual shaking with joy and anticipation, gave away her desire to grab the tub and run away with it.

There wasn't anyway we could have made any kind of decent deal with the owner for what the tub was really worth if we didn't just walk away from it right then and talk it over for a while.

It took all the strength Kelly and I had to just get my Sister's feet to start moving and walk away from that tub. We stopped shortly a little way down the walkway there we debated about if the tub was really worth the asking price and most importantly did we have enough money to buy it at this point in time, but the whole time we were talking Beanie was steadily turning her head around backwards trying not to loose sight of the tub. The fear of someone else getting it right out from under her nose was too much for her to bear. It seemed like hours before Kelly came back to us with the good news that the vendor had accepted our last dime for his old tub, and told us how we would have to go around the city just to get to where we could load it up and take it home. Beanie almost ran back to the tub and there she stood guard. You have to understand, this is how I saw the tub. First of all it was sitting all lopsided leaning to one side with the two feet that were broken off just lying down inside the tub basin. It came with its own supply of rust spots, water stains, mud

193

on its feet and last but not least wet bird feathers. Lord only knows what it had been used for previous to my Sister's arrival.

Now to get it home. It wasn't that hard to move it from the bed of one truck to the bed of ours, sort of a piece of cake, but the further down the road we went the more we thought about how we were going to get it out of our truck once we got home and exactly where were we going to put it once we got there. It couldn't go in her house with it in less that mint condition, so the decision was made to leave it outside under the carport. With that decided the fun part had just begun. Kelly wielded the two broken feet back together with homemade braces all the while trying to closely match the missing pieces. We all sandblasted the bottom, scrubbed and wire brushed the whole outside until it could be primed and painted. Once the bottom was finished it was shipped off to get the inside done. A few hundred dollars and a few hernias later the tub came back. As the refinishers were trying to get it inside Beanie's trailer the reality hit that maybe it would take a whole lot more people to do that job, so outside it stayed until she called in the troops.

I have never seen a white elephant until I looked out my front door and saw her tub sitting in front of her trailer on four legs waiting patiently for a herd of people to come and lift it inside to her bathroom at the far end of her abode. It was lacking a tail, ears and a trunk, but that didn't stop me from seeing the resemblance.

For as you see, I have my impossible dream in the form of my short stories, with this being one of them. My Sister has her impossible dream all white and shinny, patiently waiting in her bathroom for the hot water to be connected. My Sister swears that all she has done to her tub is clean and rub it ever so gently, but if you ask me I would tell you that I can't be absolutely sure she hasn't bent over and given her frog prince of a tub a kiss just to turn her dream tub into a real prince, especially when no one around was looking. The answer to your next question is **YES** I have kissed my book and I continue to do so from time to time, usually when no one around is looking.

End of Story

If You Cut Me Do I Not Bleed?

A SHORT REFLECTION

By all rights I should not be here to write this story. By all rights I should have died at the age of 16. Not because of some accident or some dreaded horribly fatal disease, no I should have died so many years ago, just simply from shear thoughts of sadness.

Very few people can fathom what it would take for someone like me to end my own life, where in reality it isn't what it would take at all; instead it all boils down to not being able to have something that you think you just simply cannot live without.

At 16 you are not burdened by mounting debt, you are not worried about Cancer, so what possibly could be the reason for such desperation at such a very tender age? Don't laugh when I tell you my first brush with death was over a man. Suicides in teenagers are almost always over failed relationships. So you would think that if I survived my first attempt, and grew up a little bit and then moved on with my life that I would see the error in my ways and never try to kill myself again. No such luck, instead the older I got, the better at the attempts I became, I guess practice does tend to make perfect.

Part of the problem with people who want to take their own lives is that they do not fear death. They have no "will to survive at all cost", like the majority of mankind does. You will never find me struggling or fighting for every breath that I take. I know that my death will be one that I either do not see coming, or it will come as a split second decision on my part to sacrifice my life for the sake of someone else's. That was a promise I made to My Mother, and that is a promise I will take to my grave.

The ones that are born with the inherent survival instinct think that the very few suicide survivors, like me, who do not fight off death tooth and nail, are doomed to eternal Hell or at least to spend eternity in limbo land somewhere on earth, which is a very far cry from Heaven. That maybe true, but that still isn't enough of a threat to put a stop to the countless number of successful suicides that occur each and ever day in every country around the globe. I believe that just like with sexual preferences, you will find that all of us are either born with the will to survive or we are born without it, and you are therefore left with very little choice in the matter.

Never in all my attempts at suicide did I take into consideration the people who do love me each and everyday, all I seemed to focus on were the ones who didn't. The last time sadness swallowed me up and the thoughts of endlessness overtook me, was with the death of my little Brother. I called my Mom and she got my other Brother to keep me talking on the phone until she and my Uncle Daddy could arrive at my house and talk me out of the strong thoughts that I had to join my little Brother in his journey into death. I was 35 at that time, which is more than double the age of 16. I know I will see the ones I love again as soon as my job on this earth is over. It seems funny now, but I can remember making a bet with my Mom and telling her that I wouldn't live past the age of 25. I guess I lost that bet, and so I'm here to tell you that when the time comes for me to swing death's bat, you won't see me hesitate to step up to that plate and play ball, because I do not share your fear of death.

THE FOR AS YOU SEE TALES

For as you see, when the time comes for someone to step forward and take a bullet for mankind, I guarantee you, the person who lays down their life for a stranger like you, will be a person who looks a lot like me.

End of Story

It Is Only A Dream

A True Story

Haven't you ever wondered why sometimes upon wakening you find that you are able to tell what you just dreamed to everyone around you? Then at other times what you have just dreamed will be instantly forgotten the second you pour your first morning cup of coffee and sit down into your easy chair to drink it. Some dreams are so real to you that you will awaken visibly shaking from the feeling you have just experienced as you dreamed you have been falling helplessly towards the ground. I am not really sure who said that if you do not wake up before you dream you hit the ground then you will die in your sleep. How that statement can be proven or disproved will never be known to man, only the spirit in us and in our dreams will know if that statement is true or false. All I can say for sure is I have never failed to awaken before putting my dreams of hitting the ground and surviving to the ultimate test.

Nothing out of the ordinary happened that day to bring on the dream and nothing out of the ordinary was expected from that night's sleep, so what I am about to tell you came totally as a surprise to me, and I remember this dream as if it has happened every night since.

The door to the cargo hold of this airplane was open wide, and the altitude that the plane was flying was just about cloud level with the ground coming in and out of view. The plane's airspeed I would estimate to be approximately 500 miles per hour with a good view of cars as they slowly drove down the highway beneath the plane like ants moving under my feet. The door being opened didn't upset me much because at that time I really wasn't afraid of heights and I was more interested in taking in the view. As I stood there looking out the door I caught sight of a man coming out of the shadows from a far corner of the cargo hold, just where the sunlight shinning in stops and the darkness of the plane's interior begins. He didn't have to introduce himself for me to know who he was, even though it was the first time I had come face to face with him, Satan's presence can not be mistaken.

He wasn't mean, he wasn't nasty, and he wasn't rude, but he was very calm and forceful when he said, "You will have to jump out of this plane,—but I am going to give you a choice. You can either jump out without a parachute or you can jump with a parachute that I can give to you." I asked, "What do I have to do to get a parachute from you?" The Devil replied, "I will give you one, if upon jumping, you give your soul to me." There was no hesitation on my part, and as I jumped from the plane, I just said one word, and that one word was, "NO".

Waking up from that dream was the best feeling I could have ever had and I still rejoice in the fact that I said "NO" when I was put to the test. I truly believe that if I had put out my hand and touched the parachute that he was offering me then I would never have awakened from that dream.

You see the Devil makes promises he never intends to keep, and if we are not to be given a choice as to what happens to our eternal souls then why does the Devil have to use so much of his "power of temptation" to try and lead us astray? What if our souls are won or lost not in a conscious state of mind, but deep down somewhere in our **subconscious dream state** instead?

For as you see, what if, (lets just say for instance) what if, when it becomes Judgment Day and you are waiting to see if you will get the thumbs up or the thumbs down at heaven's gate, what do you think you would do if suddenly you find out that which way you end up going rested totally upon a choice you made in a dream you just had the night before? Would it be the ultimate gift or would it be the ultimate bummer?

End of Story

My Wet Suit

A SHORT STORY

You would think from the title of this story that it would be about some great undersea adventure; nope this story involves a few really big Mountains instead of a really big Ocean.

It was all planned in advance, and the correct deposits were sent to reserve our full day of snowmobile fun once we arrived in Jackson, WY. Our winter vacation ended up being scheduled too early for skiing. Since it was the off season for skiing we were a little bit concerned whether or not there would be enough snow for us to have a good time, and so for about the whole month of November I worried if the snow would even be there when we landed in Jackson. Kelly would keep check on the Internet weather web site almost daily to get an extended forecast for Jackson and the Yellowstone area. As the time for our flight grew nearer, the anticipation of seeing snow was better than any Christmas present we could have received this year.

The plane ride was tiring because of the three take offs and landings we had to make just to get there, but once we got our feet on the snow we quickly forgot about all the trouble and just enjoyed watching the snow flakes hit our noses. I had ridden on a snowmobile with Kelly at the wheel a couple of years before this, and so we once again picked the same tour group, but this time it would be a little bit different because I would be driving my own snowmobile. You have to remember that I do not even drive the riding lawnmower at my house so driving a snowmobile definitely was going to be a first for me.

It all starts with you putting on underwear, then you put on thermal underwear, and then a shirt and blue jeans, and then a sweater, finally you top it off of course with your coat. The tour group picks you up at the hotel you are staying at and takes you to their office. When you finally get to where you are ready to suit up for the trip, the tour group furnishes you with a one-piece snowmobile suit, boots, gloves, and a helmet.

Now if you can still stand up and walk after getting all that on, then you are fed a good breakfast, loaded into a heated van and drove way out of town to whichever of the three trips you have signed up for.

We chose the one to Granite Hot Springs. It is a great trip with you snowmobiling 10 miles into a canyon that has a swimming pool fed by a natural hot spring coming straight out of the side of a Mountain. After getting to swim in the pool and being fed a great steak cookout meal, you snowmobile back to the van and then they take you back to the office to get out of your garb. Last but not least you go back to your hotel with a day full of memories and fun.

Just leave it to me to add a little bit more action to a very well planned snowmobile trip. It went great right up until the moment the snowmobiles started cranking up and the guide pointed to a little port-a-potty and said that if anyone needed to go, they had better go now, because it would be a while before we would reach the next port-a-potty. Luckily I had just went to the bathroom right after eating breakfast, but I also had made the mistake of drinking more coffee than I should have, and it was just about then that the coffee caught up with me and my bladder. I tried to be the last person to visit the port-a-potty, and so when my Sister came out I hurried in after her and made her stand guard right outside the toilet since the door wouldn't stay shut. I kept saying, "Beanie holds the door" over and over again until she reassured me that she would.

It was painstakingly hard to remove all the clothing necessary to get the job done, but somehow I managed to get all of them down, well I have to say I just thought I had cleared all the clothes from the toilet seat. It wasn't until I didn't hear the sound of urine hitting the bottom of the bucket that I realized it was going somewhere besides the potty. I looked down and there it was the collar to my snowmobile suit in perfect position under the seat. My worse fears had been confirmed the collar had acted like a sponge and all I could do about it was say, "Oh Man", that was when my Sister said, "What's wrong?"

When I emerged from the potty and told her the whole story, I thought she would never stop laughing at my predicament and me. Sometimes you just have to play the hand that is dealt to you and this was one of those times. My wet suit and I jumped on the snowmobile and acted like nothing had ever happened.

My Sister and I looked at one another and with all our thumbs up we said, "**It's All Good**". The trip was so wonderful and amazing that nothing could have ruined it for us.

For as you see, it wasn't until I pulled my wet suit down to my waist and climbed into the seat of the van for our trip back to town that I remembered what had happened at the start of our journey. Don't worry the wet suit got a bath when we got back to the office and I, myself, made sure I took two baths at the hotel before I felt clean enough to go any further. Snowmobile Vacation of "03" will be one etched into my memory, because you know what "**It's All Good**".

End of Story

Paul, Are There Really Any Angels?

A SHORT STORY

This is a question I started to ask one day, but before I could get the words out of my mouth, several events happened to make the question a mute point. One event was the one where my 18 yr. old niece (Lauren) called me and her Mom (my Sister) Beanie, crying because she had swerved out of the fast lane of I-20 to try and miss a dead dog which caused her to lose control of her car, and then cross three lanes of traffic ending up in the dirt along side the hwy. When I came up on the scene the first thought that crossed my mind was "how in the world did she manage to not flip the car over, or even worse get hit by any on coming cars?" The ground was wet and the incline she came to a stop on was pretty steep so it would have been very easy just to roll the car over and over again. She wasn't hurt only shook up and frightened, so Beanie decided to stay with her and drive the rest of the day. That was miracle number one.

Miracle number two happened that same day in that very same car only a couple of hours later. This time I receive another phone call from my sister telling me that she and Lauren had just gotten hit from behind this time and the car was totaled. When I came upon the second wreck of the day for Lauren, the first thought that crossed my mind was "How did the car keep from bursting into flames?" The whole rear end was crushed into the back seat, with the gas tank exposed and very visible when you looked at the back of the car. Luckily no one was in the back seat at the time of impact.

For as you see, to answer your question, "Are there really any Angels?" The answer to that question is, "Just as the Devil has his Demons, **THE GOOD LORD** has his <u>ANGELS</u>. So there can't be any doubt in your mind when I tell you that your very special **MOM** is now one of GOD'S chosen GUARDIAN ANGELS sent to watch over you."

End of Story

This Is What's Wrong With This World

A SHORT STORY

For as you see, what is wrong with this world is all the things you can't see or hear that is happening around us at any given time. It is all the violence, hate, evil, abuse, and neglect people bestow on one another. Unfortunately you will not be able to fully realize exactly "**what is wrong with this world**" until it comes into your own front yard and stands at your own front door. That's why this story is in honor of 9/11/01, the day evil came and knocked at our front door.

End of Story

The Way I See It...

A PERSONAL REFECTION

March 11, 2011... A massive 8.9-magnitude quake hit northeast **Japan.** It was on a Friday. What was I doing at that time? I really couldn't tell you, but what I can tell you is that this is just the beginning.

When will man open up his eyes, and read the signs? Or is it already too late? At what point in time did it become too late to stop what is written in Revelations?

So many questions with so little time left to give anyone answers to these questions. It was once said, "Only GOD can make a tree". I wish that statement was still true today. With mankind cloning this and cloning that, he has upset the natural balance of this planet. There are hybrid plants and animals being made by man each and everyday by splitting atoms and DNA to make this planet a so called "better place" to live on. Well somewhere down the line man has crossed over into a realm in which he was never suppose to enter. Somewhere in time, probably when man first started making test tube babies, man found himself beginning to play GOD.

Even if man had never mutated any of the things on this planet; the least thing that man has done is move the different animals and insects around to different continents, so that now man finds out that the things that he chose to relocate no longer have any natural enemies to keep them in check, so what does man do? You guessed it, he moves their natural enemies around also. Lord when will it ever end? Well in my opinion it already has moved closer to the time of saying goodbye to this planet and that time is on a down hill ride gaining speed with each day that passes.

So how do you go back to putting things right again? The whole island of Japan is going to have to be evacuated. Shut down all Nuclear Power Plants. Stop industrializing every city. Leave the plants and animals alone and stop killing the bugs, which in turn end up killing the bees and birds that eat those bugs.

Have you noticed the key word in what I am suggesting is the word, "STOP"?

For as you see, In my opinion will mankind ever STOP, I really, really doubt it. Not until the end of this planet makes him stop. Where will we go from there? Well if there is still any ice left on the North and South Poles then that would be the place I would suggest for mankind to go. Why there, you ask, well, Ice is the one place germs can't grow, Ice can be melted down into a fresh water supply, oh and last but not least, Ice will be my climate of choice to try and avoid the global warming that will occur once all the Nuclear Power Plants melt down. It sounds really grim I know, but if you take the time to read a little bit of the Book of Revelations, then you will know what is in store for us all, and none of it, I am sorry to say, is a bed of roses.

End of Story

Why I Cry At Christmas

A SHORT STORY

For a long time now I really have not liked Christmas, and for the life of me I couldn't figure out why the Holiday Season had become such a bad time of year for me. It wasn't until recently that I decided to sit down and try to figure out exactly when I had made the turn around from looking forward to Christmas each year to just simply dreading it.

It wasn't because of the over crowding in the stores or the dead line you have to meet, none of that has changed over the half century since the day I was born. My Mom had always made Christmas a joy for all her kids each year and she never showed any preference from one child to the other, she loved all of her kids equally, each one of the four of us had a special place in her heart we could call our own, so where and what had caused the change in me?

I had to begin my quest for answers by putting all the events in my life on a history time line and then chart them out. I started by trying to estimate at what point in time I started turning into a small Scrooge totally equipped with my own "BAH HUM BUG", and

THE FOR AS YOU SEE TALES

when I did chart the events, a little light actually went off inside my head. The first event that I charted occurred on 1/26/84 and then the second was 10/07/87 and the last happened one year ago today 12/23/02 two days before Christmas. It seems like the reason I no longer care for Christmas is because things that always make me cry happen really close to that most precious of Holiday Seasons. My Father passed away of a heart attack, then my little Brother died suddenly of an aneurysm in his head, and then last year I had to tell my Mom she had Cancer and was only given 3 to 6 more months to live. None of these things could have been changed and none of them were of my own doing, but still all of them make me cry deeply and send me spiraling into that all familiar deep dark pit of depression.

I use to think it was what they call Seasonal Affective Disorder or (SAD) where there isn't enough sun light hours providing light to your eyes. That reasoning almost made sense to me up until the event time line came along, now I finally know the real reason for my tears at Christmas.

Just so you will know, the only man who was ever a Father to me, my Uncle Daddy, Paul Thompson, passed away early **Christmas** morning this last Christmas 2004, so this Christmas will bring even more special tears to my eyes. All my loved ones, that I miss dearly, have to go away at what should be a time of "Joy and Peace for all", but it just doesn't seem to hold that much "Joy or Peace" for me this year.

For as you see, now that I know the real reason for my tears, I finally developed a different mind set towards the Joy of Christmas for me and all those around me. Merry Christmas and a Happy New Year from me to you, given out just one year at a time, you never know what next Christmas will send my way.

End of Story

For Mrs. Carson, a special Christmas Lady.

Is There A Weight Limit In Heaven?

A SHORT STORY

My how time flies when you are not having fun. I had it right in the palm of my hand and then just like I seem to always do, I let it slip away again. I'll try not to keep you in the dark any longer; I know you will be just as disappointed in me as I am in myself when I tell you that I still weight as much now as I ever did 3 yrs ago. That to me means another three years wasted, three years that could have added considerably to my life expectancy. I started trying to improve my health by losing weight on 1/2/05 and by the time 5/20/05 came along I had lost down to 188lbs which amounted to 45 lbs of total loss. I went down in pants sizes and up in self-esteem. It didn't take much for me to quit trying to get healthier, in fact I was probably looking for any reason big or small to help me quit. It is a whole lot easier to remain obese than it ever is to get thin. I found out that I am my own worst enemy.

THE FOR AS YOU SEE TALES

Have you ever looked around and seen how many things have weight limits? You can't put but so many people in a boat and if all of them are adults over 200 lbs; then you are limited even more so. There are limits on occupancy for elevators, planes, and golf carts. I hate to get on a crowded elevator, because I think I just might be the one that causes the breaks to fail. Did you know that there is a weight limit of 200 lbs if you want to ride the mules down into the Grand Canyon? Well that leaves me out, how about you? All I can say is thank God someone is looking out for the poor mules.

I truly believe that the weight people lose doesn't go anywhere. Think about it, if I lose 5 lbs isn't there someone somewhere on this planet gaining those same 5 lbs? How could the world possible survive if everyone everywhere lost weight all at the same time? What would happen to the planet if no one died but yet babies were still being born? The added weight to the surface of the planet would have to compress it at its core level making all the volcanoes start erupting more often.

Which makes me even more concerned about all the heavy metals and oil that we are steadily rising to the surface. OK OK, no more gloom and doom, my point is I want to save myself from an early wheelchair and /or grave and I know that limiting my weight to a normal level is the best way to save my knees and my pride at the same time losing weight will bring my blood pressure back under control. Nothing but a plus plus.

For as you see, if there really is a weight limit in heaven then I plan on making that just one less thing I have to worry about when the time comes for me to weigh in at those pearly gates.

End of Story

Divorce

ONE OF LIFE'S LITTLE ADVENTURES

It is hard for me to remember back 40 years to the day I married Mr. Cox. Honestly for the most part it has been a grand 40 years, come to think of it. I must say that there has been only one time that brought me to the point of considering leaving my husband and that is a story in and of itself.

We had taken a vacation with my Sister and Niece all the way up to Yellowstone. On our way back home for Jackson Hole, WY for some reason Mr. Cox decided to sit, and drive all that day without saying one word to me. His only crime was keeping his mouth shut, go figure. As the trip progressed and the miles ticked by, I became more and more Pissed Off at him. So when we arrived at our stopping point for the night, I told Mr. Cox he would not be eating supper with us, so he stayed outside. After ordering food my Sister asked me to give her a percentage. She said, "What percent of the time do you enjoy being with him?" My answer to that question was 90 percent of the time. She gave me the strangest look and said, "You mean to tell me, you would leave a perfectly good man just for

THE FOR AS YOU SEE TALES

10 percent of the time." I laughed when I told her she was right. That was when I got up and went outside to find Mr. Cox still sitting on a street corner in Amarillo.

For as you see, with increasing age comes increasing intolerance, but in my case, the good does still outweigh the bad even though if you asked me now the same question that was asked of me in Amarillo, I would have to say my answer to that question would have to be 80 percent now. He has never done that stunt again. LOL, SUCH IS LIFE.

End of Story

What Is "FAMILY"?

A REALLY SHORT STORY

You know I still have an Aunt on my father's side of my "FAMILY" that is living. Even though I haven't gone to see her in, what one would say is a lifetime, I still know that if I showed up on her door step unexpected that she would welcome me into her house with open arms. That little trip to see my Aunt and Uncle should be one of the things that I am putting on my bucket list now that Kelly, me and my Sister are all retired and have all the time in the world to sit down and go visit with them.

Families <u>do not</u> have to spend every holiday with each other and families <u>do not</u> have to have a really close bond to feel the love that they share for one another. All a family has to know is that when the time comes, and push comes to shove that their family will be there for them; come hell or high water.

For as you see, it was two "FAMILIES" that put a definition to all the words that we now know. I have got to tell you though, when it came to defining the meaning of the word "FAMILY" it was definitely more of an undertaking for the two families to do than they could ever have imagined. Look it up, the meaning of the word "FAMILY" just goes on and on and on, and I am sure my family, "as odd as they are", do fit in there somewhere!

Is a family member, made by an act of marriage, any less of a family member to you than one that became part of your family upon the day they were born?

The answer to that question lies only in one's own heart. Personally, in my heart, **they are all created equal.**

End of Story

For Fabrin

Love Means Never Having To Say You're Sorry

A PERSONAL REFLECTION

Was it a perfect love story? At the time I saw it I would have to give it a YES.

I have always watched shows that seem to end in tragedy. With "Romeo and Juliet" being the one that tops my tragedy list. Mainly because of the time I saw it. It came out on the silver screen at a very impressionable age for me, because turning from a puberty grub into a beautiful butterfly was a monumental chore. Stretching my wings in an effort to learn to fly away was very hard for me to do. This ugly duckling didn't want to turn into a beautiful swan. Hahaha. Eventually hormones did kick in, and independence finally arose to shove me out of the nest.

My love life was one bad road trip after another. Then along came my "Prince Charming". He was not all bright and shinny with pearly white teeth and a teddy bear personality, but most soul mates aren't. Under his rough outer facade I saw my Romeo. He

THE FOR AS YOU SEE TALES

has been a daily work in progress for me. If I had a nickel for all the blood, sweat, and tears it took me to keep him headed in the right direction, then I could give Donald T. a run for his money, and be the first women president. I know if I ran against Donald, I would get at least one vote, being the one I would get coming from my Sister. He tweets, she fusses. Now that is just way past funny. Time to get to the point.

For as you see, why is death sometimes the only way to achieve forgiveness?

Case point, Jesus said, "FATHER, FORGIVE THEM" and then he died. What I find interesting about that is, he didn't ask his Father to forgive "him", and that was simply because he knew his Father's love meant he <u>never had to say</u> he was sorry. Where there is LOVE, forgiveness should always be (a given). Time can heal all wounds, but first you have to be willing to <u>sign</u> the consent form in front of you in order to let it.

End of Story

Debridement (AKA) Picking A Scab

MY STORY

A few months back my husband, of 42yrs, developed an abscess on his leg in what a lot of people would call his "nether regions". My Sister is an RN, and very capable of doctoring it up for him, but since it was in his "no fly zone" that was just not going to happen.

I wasn't really sure that the lump he found on his leg didn't involve his groin lymph glands, so for that reason I decided to take him to the VA emergency room to be seen by a physician. It didn't take long before the surgeons were called down to the ER to decide what needed to be done about his leg lump. I was able to stay with him as one of the surgeons explained what was involved in prepping, deadening, and opening up the area of deep seeded infection. As I sat there I could see my husbands mind tumbling over and over again saying to himself, (this just can't be good). Hahaha

I would have given anything if I could have been in the room as the procedure was being done. Luckily I wasn't because I would still be laughing at him and the situation that he found himself caught up in. He was trapped and he knew it.

My husband told me, on our way home, exactly what had happened to him once I was asked to leave him and go have a seat in the ER waiting room until they finished the debridement procedure. Let me tell you how he described it.

The procedure started with two surgeons, one on each side of the exam table/bed he was lying on. After setting up the tray with sterile syringes, sponges, hemostats and other assorted tools of the trade, they went to work on my husband's leg. After the first numbing injection took affect he really didn't feel that much more pain, which was a good thing.

Then all of a sudden he started noticing that the bed he was lying on was slowly moving, and then slowly but surely he felt himself start sliding down to the bottom of the bed. This was while the two surgeons were still cutting and draining his leg. At first it was a mystery why the bed was moving, but then it became quite evident. It really was not a ghost in the room causing him to rise up into a sitting position. No, it was the main surgeon accidentally stepping on a bed control foot pedal next to the surgeon's foot.

The main surgeon on his case apologized for accidentally stepping on the bed control foot pedal. All was forgiven when it came to the mishap, but the procedure wasn't over with yet. As things progressed, my husband once again started feeling himself slowly moving into a sitting position on the exam table/bed. The same surgeon that had told him he was sorry the first time had to turn right back around, and apologize for the second fopa as well. You see lightening does seem to be able to strike twice in one place. Hahaha

Once I got him home I had to make sure the wound stayed clean, dry, and packed with gauze for a week until his next follow-up visit. Changing bandages was not a problem, but removing the packing gauze, and then repacking the wound daily turned out to be somewhat more of a challenge. I knew that if the surgeons had left any of the infection in the wound, and closed it up with sutures, or let a scab start growing over the wound; then the enclosed infection could have caused my husband blood poisoning and then he would become septic. The blood poisoning, in some cases could result in eventual death. All's well that ends well is what they say, and to be honest the scar from his ordeal can barely be seen, except of course, only by me using a magnifying glass. **ROTFL**.

For as you see, some fresh wounds can just be sewed up immediately and then they will heal, but deep seeded wounds that are already infected can only heal if they are kept open. They need to heal slowly from the inside out. A heart wound is exactly the same way. If it hasn't healed in 2 yrs then just closing the wound back up again and ignoring it will not bring about any of the needed healing. Laughter has been known to be the best medicine to jump start any healing. If you hurt yourself, "do the dance of the wild monkey", and then laugh as you shake off the pain.

What about the scar that is left by picking at the heart, you ask? Well fresh wound or old wound, the scar left behind will be exactly the same. The wound must be allowed to air out, and be kept open with communication by both parties until it decides to heal.

The healing properties of debridement can be felt by all those whose hearts have been wounded. <u>Thank God</u> my heart is not a slow healer. Just **FYI** and **LOL**. Your choice.

End of Story

Funny Is In The Eyes Of The Beholder

A SHORT STORY

I can't tell you when it happened to me, or why it happened. Maybe it happened when I was dropped on my head shortly after birth. Maybe it happened when I almost drowned myself around the age of 3, or maybe it came about on simply the day I was born. Who knows? All I know is that I have a very different sense of humor compared to all my other siblings, and most of all the other people whose path I have had the pleasure to come across.

If I only had a penny for every time I was told, "that's not funny" my name would be on top of the list of billionaires. See to me that comment I just said is even funny. Ok, Ok I am a little bit off track here, so let's get back to my story. Hahaha, let me know if you find and get the humor in this one. OK

I remember very little about my childhood, but I do remember the events of this day quite clearly.

Mom had decided to take me and my little Sister to the public swimming pool for our days outing. It would be her way to relax and still be able to watch me splash around in the kiddy end of the pool. My sister was too little to even walk around good let alone play unattended, so Momma kept a tight grip on her at all times. I had to have been around 3 years of age and my little Sister, who is 1yr and nine days younger than me, had to have been around 2 at that time.

Mom was sitting on the kiddy pool steps holding me on one of her knees and my little Sister was sitting on her other knee with both of Mom's knees just barely above water level. Lord knows what I was thinking when I all of a sudden left the safety of her knee and I sank right to the bottom of the pool. If I had just stood up then my head would have been above the water level, but nope, I just sat there with my eyes wide open. It was the first time my head had ever gone under water. I was in shock I guess or maybe I didn't know exactly what I needed to do next, so I just sat there.

The only one that was in distress over the situation was my Mom. It took only seconds before she realized that I wasn't coming up for air. As she reached down into the water to save me, she dropped my Sister off her other knee and now she had both her kids with their heads under water. When she finally got us both back up on her knee and safely out of the water; she had two very wet, balling their eyes out, babies to deal with. So much for a day of rest and relaxation.

Guess who had to start taking swimming lessons at the ripe old age of 3, you guessed it, it was me. I still know how to swim, but I will always hold my nose if I think there is even the slightest of chances that my head will go under water, and I make a point to stay at the shallow end of the pool. Lesson learned. Hope you saw the humor in that story, but if you didn't, then I have more you can read over until you do. Hahaha

For as you see, you can receive a liver transplant. You can even receive a kidney transplant, and maybe one day you will be able to

THE FOR AS YOU SEE TALES

wake up with a new brain. But there is just one thing for certain; you are stuck with the **funny bone** you were born with.

Now that is just way past funny. That statement deserves an encore. Hahaha Thank You Thank You Very Much...Kathy has left the building.

End of Story

I Surrender

A SHORT STORY

Two best friends just happen to have joined the army right at the same time a war broke out. As they sat on their bunks in boot camp each of them looked at the other and said, "What have we gotten our selves into? Well at least if we go down fighting this war, then we will be going down together".

After basic training; off they went to fight a war that should never have been started. What they were told was that this war was being fought for democracy in a foreign land. Democracy is worth fighting for only if it is your democracy, and what you want to shed your own blood for. That wasn't the case for these two soldiers, but still they went off to war in the name of "justice".

Day after day the two soldiers would go and take a hill from their enemy, and the very next day their enemy would win it back. Tired and hungry the two would sit in their tents thinking out loud, "What day is this? How many times have we taken this hill? Why can't we just move onto another hill and take it instead?" I know it wasn't funny, but the two of them were too tired to do much more

THE FOR AS YOU SEE TALES

than laugh it off, and go back out and fight to reclaim the hill once again.

It is pride that keeps the war and blood shed going. The generals and presidents know that the loser of their war will have to go on television and the internet to give their public the reason the war they chose to fight ended in their defeat. None of the leaders are willing to surrender the battle and in turn declare their losses. If the leaders of the wars were placed on the battle field standing face to face at the front lines, then all wars would be ended the first day that they were fought. It would be the shortest war ever fought in the history books, just think of all the people that could be saved if wars were started and fought that way.

After all he is our "commander and chief", why not see if he is able to fight as well as he leads the country.

For as you see, it will be the better man who is the first one to raise and wave the white flag. As soon as we leave the foreign lands we fought on; democracy will be flying back home with us. In the seat right next to ours on the same plane.

Battles fought over seas will never be won by just us alone. Take for example "Desert Storm" did we win that one? I am still confused about that outcome.

End of Story

My Swan Song

MY HOW TIME FLIES WHEN YOU ARE HAVING FUN!!!

It has been 15 years since I wrote my first book. I have the money needed to put this second book into publication as well. The money is here today, but will it be there tomorrow? Good question and if past events are an indicator of what the future holds for me then one thing is certain, the money may be here today, but it probably will be gone by tomorrow. Never delay getting something done or when you go back to get it, with money in your hand, you will find that you were just 5 minutes too late to get that most wonderful recliner at that most wonderful Saturday Estate Sale you just left behind.

Granted this book could have used a few more stories in it to make it equal to my first book, but I have always gone for quality over quantity. There will be more stories written by me; I am certain; before my eyes close for good, but there will never be another book undertaking started by me. I had to come to the reality that even

THE FOR AS YOU SEE TALES

though my mind is young and willing to play games with the little ones; my body is failing me on a daily basis.

The Tree's embers finally went out 12/31/2014. The fire burned for 12 years before it finally took down the Tree. Sadly, all I could do was sit down and watch it burn. What can you do with the ashes left behind once a tree is burned down? There are a lot of uses for ashes. You can de-skunk your pets by rubbing a handful of ashes on your dog's coat which will then neutralize the skunk's odor. It can hide stains on your driveway. Enrich compost material as fertilizer decomposes. Block garden pests from eating your plants. Melt ice, control pond algae, make your tomatoes grow, and clean glass. My point is even though the Tree is gone, and you though it would stand for thousand of years like the Great General Grant Sequoia Tree, absolutely nothing last forever.

I will leave you on a high note as I start this second book's journey...No better way to end this book!

End of book, but **definitely not** end of stories.

ABOUT THE AUTHOR

About the Author is a story within a story. There are stories that make me cry and then there are stories even I can't believe could have come from within me, but even so, I have to say that no one but myself can take the blame for all this mess. Once again I have taken the journey to see this book through to its completion, but sadly I can't help but wonder why I am taking this journey. I can't help but wonder "why me?" All I can figure out is that when I end up in a nursing home one day; as I know I will; that maybe reading my stories to all my fellow nursing home friends will make the time I have left pass by just a little bit more slowly.

At any rate, there are some really good stories and then there are some not so good. To each his own. My favorite story in my first book was "Genie In A Bottle" and my favorite one in this book is "Smelling The Roses"? If you look deep enough I know you will find a story you can call your favorite too. Thank you for reading them – Yours Always-Kathy (AE) Cox

CPSIA information can be obtained
at www.ICGtesting.com
Printed in the USA
BVHW032257251019
562124BV00002B/2/P